KU-499-367

GORSKY

GORSKY

Vesna Goldsworthy

Chatto & Windus
LONDON

Published by Chatto & Windus 2015

2 4 6 8 10 9 7 5 3 1

Copyright © Vesna Goldsworthy 2015

Vesna Goldsworthy has asserted her right under the Copyright, Designs
and Patents Act 1988 to be identified as the author of this work.

This book is sold subject to the condition that it shall not,
by way of trade or otherwise, be lent, resold, hired out,
or otherwise circulated without the publisher's prior
consent in any form of binding or cover other than that
in which it is published and without a similar condition,
including this condition, being imposed
on the subsequent purchaser.

First published in Great Britain in 2015 by
Chatto & Windus
Penguin Random House, 20 Vauxhall Bridge Road,
London SW1V 2SA

www.randomhouse.co.uk

A Penguin Random House Company

Penguin
Random House
UK

Addresses for companies within The Random House Group Limited can be found at:
www.randomhouse.co.uk/offices.htm

The Random House Group Limited Reg. No. 954009

A CIP catalogue record for this book
is available from the British Library

ISBN 9781784740092

The Random House Group Limited supports the Forest Stewardship Council® (FSC®),
the leading international forest-certification organisation. Our books carrying the
FSC label are printed on FSC®-certified paper. FSC is the only forest-certification
scheme supported by the leading environmental organisations, including Greenpeace.
Our paper procurement policy can be found at: www.randomhouse.co.uk/environment

Typeset in Adobe Garamond by Palimpsest Book Production Limited,
Falkirk, Stirlingshire
Printed and bound in Great Britain by
Clays Ltd, St Ives plc

For Jacqueline Lewis

Such was the report which the English legations made of what they had seen and suffered in Russia; and their evidence was confirmed by the appearance which the Russian legations made in England. The strangers spoke no civilised language. Their garb, their gestures, their salutations, had a wild and barbarous character. The ambassador and the grandees who accompanied him were so gorgeous that all London crowded to stare at them, and so filthy that nobody dared to touch them. They came to the court balls dropping pearls and vermin.

Thomas Macaulay, *The History of England* (1848)

1

It was a piece of business that comes along once in a lifetime. If you are lucky.

First there was a year of glamorous parties: an unexpected, undeserved year, unlike anything I had ever experienced. Then it all suddenly stopped and I had to return to what I was before, to a different language and a different place. Gorsky changed my life.

I remember his first visit to the shop. You couldn't fail to notice him, even in a city like London, in which millions are bent on attracting attention. People walk around with exhibitionist swagger, as though starring in their own YouTube clip. He was quietly remarkable: foreign,

expensive, somehow still even when he moved, his volume turned down permanently. His melancholy muzzle was equine and aristocratic, and his tailored worsteds so ripely English that at first I thought he could only be Prussian.

A lot of redundant Deutsche princes dabble in antiques and art in these reaches of Knightsbridge and Chelsea. They often punch above their meagre monetary weight when it comes to tailoring, these von Thises and von Thats. He possessed billions, more money than anyone can surely spend, let alone need, in a lifetime. He dressed the part, too, but you had to look closely to notice it. His money did not shout. It whispered in the rustle of whitest Egyptian cotton, finest cashmere and softest calfskin, and in the ticking of the most precise platinum watch mechanism ever made. He had so many more or less identical Savile Row suits that they must have been as disposable as tissue paper: I don't imagine he bothered with dry-cleaning. And although I used to spend half my life staring out of the shop window, trying to guess the birthplace of each occasional passer-by, Russia did not even cross my mind. It's not so much that his hyperborean blondness did not fit

the frozen marshes of the Neva estuary. Something more intangible about the set of his features directed me towards old Königsberg. Narrow and chiselled like a tall crystal vase, with blue eyes set a touch too near his long straight nose, his face made him look taller than he was, and like a creature from another era – Ernst Jünger's best mate, a wandering Balt, or Byron's Germanic pen pal painted from the back by Caspar Friedrich, turning slowly towards the viewer with some profound insight about the frozen sea he had been gazing at a minute before.

The Russians looked tougher, beefier and coarser, even when they were undeniably handsome. I don't mean Russians in general, of course, but the Russians in this handful of London's richest postcodes, that self-selected set of men belonging to the generation which in the West would have been called baby-boomers. In Russia, their lives had spun a full circle. They grew up in shared apartments, made billions in crude oil, gas or sophisticated scams, spent it on houses, horses, whores, and occasionally hired killers, and finally returned to playing cards with each other just as they did in the bad old Communist days,

only now surrounded by squads of bodyguards. I should have guessed that he was Jewish too. But in the end his Jewishness mattered to him and Natalia Summerscale more than it mattered to me. They were Russian. I am not.

I am from a small and insignificant nation in an insignificant corner of Europe and am glad this is so. For this story my nationality matters only in the negative, only in so far as I was neither English nor Russian, and only because, after it had all happened, it was the one thing that persisted in the captions below the grainy photographs of me and him, then me alone, as though it was my defining feature, despite it being the last thing I reached for in describing myself. You could say I am tumbleweed, a species that disengages from its roots once matured. The condition of exile was not altogether unpleasant. I had chosen it for myself.

All those months in London now seem as cold as November. My recollections are vivid but they refuse to obey the calendar. England offered no seasons to anchor the memory. The rare bursts of blue could just as easily

have been furnished by Constable or Turner: you went to galleries to escape the drizzle. It rained all the time and the weather changed only when the rain turned into sleet. Once or twice, on my way to work, I raised my eyes towards the clouds that sat low over waterlogged gardens and I glimpsed a pale orb behind them; an early sun or a late moon, you couldn't tell, just hanging up there, like a thief's promise. Even mid-spring, it felt like the *beginning of next winter*, or so everyone joked. Throughout most of that unseasoned year people would walk into the shop, shudder, say something about the weather, then stare at the book spines on the shelves while they got warm or until they spied a title they wanted, inspected a copy and made a note to order it online. Although it cost eight thousand pounds a month in rent alone, Fynch's bookshop might as well have been a showroom for the internet book trade. Only a few souls would buy something, out of guilt, before walking back into the rain – a card or, if they were feeling flush, one of those slim poetry volumes which shift so few copies that the web-based outfits don't bother to reduce their prices. Even with such meagre pickings the

business perked up once the winter was allegedly over, but only just, only against our usual seasonal figures, and those were, let's face it, far from great.

Fynch's is not the kind of bookshop anyone goes to for their beach reads, unless perhaps it's a private beach. And it is definitely *off the beaten track* – the cliché has rarely been as true – tucked away in one of those side streets where there are no other shops and the footfall is minimal. Only someone who is not too keen on selling anything would bury a bookshop in a row of mews houses in the no man's land between Knightsbridge and Chelsea, the dominion of interior decorators and sleekly furnished dwellings in which coffee-table books outnumber other volumes by three to one. These are the actual numbers, by the way, not figure-of-speech ones.

There are exceptions, in 'old Chelsea'. There is no 'old Knightsbridge' any more, unless you count the first wave of Kuwaitis pushed out by the sort of people for whom oil is now less exciting as a commodity than lemon sherbets. 'Old Chelsea', however, Christopher Fynch's so-called regulars, are English right down to their M&S underwear. They fritter

away the last copper coins from their imperial petty cash in gentle ways that do include buying an occasional book. I don't necessarily prefer the 'old' to the 'new' Chelsea, with its European and North American usurpation of gentlemanly styles, but I am ethnically predisposed to be sentimental about any group of people collectively stupid enough to be pushed out of their own land. They are a dying breed, 'old Chelsea', and will soon be as extinct as their orders of biographies of Viscount Allenby or Cardinal What'shisname, and their talk of Martin Amis as a risqué young thing. Their own children prefer to look like 'new money' even when they have none.

The morning he first asked me for a quick chat, if he might – *if he might?!* – I watched him emerge from a long silver Bentley or some such vehicle, the sort of car that must be sufficiently armour-plated to withstand an anti-tank grenade attack. I did not foresee that he would turn towards Fynch's. He was hesitant and stiff, one eye partly closed while he inspected the shop sign, as though he had a monocle over the other. Though he must have purchased more than anyone else I am ever likely to meet, I don't suppose he often bothered with *shopping*. I watched him, still not quite believing that he was about to come inside, through the rain-spattered window behind which I sat for hours each day at a desk covered with handwritten receipts ('old Chelsea' loved those), under a poster that asked the patrons to support their local independent bookshop. We were independent all right. And bookish, too. In spite of the mess, which gave the appearance of frantic activity, I managed to read a couple of titles a day, even on what passed for a busy one. I certainly did not ever expect to have to deal with 'big business', and everything about this man – from the way he stepped out of the vehicle, giving brief instructions to the sharp-suited driver who held the car's door for him, to the manner in which he lingered uncertainly among the shelves as I completed a minute transaction and chatted with one of our morning regulars, and the tone in which he finally uttered that *if I might* – spelled out big business.

Morning regulars hereabouts mostly meant elderly ladies in carefully coiffed, inky-white helmets of hair, who had been up since four thirty, and who enjoyed reading stories about cultured spinsters by the likes of

Anita Brookner or Salley Vickers, and empathising fully, even though they were not spinsters themselves. Only a banker's widow can afford to live alone in this part of town, and some of these tough old birds had been multiply widowed by multiple bankers. They enjoyed talking to me, killing half an hour, before taking a lift to the top-floor cafe at Peter Jones where they killed the rest of the morning. My foreignness was an advantage in their eyes, because they liked explaining England's ways to me, although they were now as lost in England as I was. They were my best customers. They never bought books online not because they disliked the internet but because they did not even know that such a thing was possible.

I was not a gentleman bookseller, although I made some efforts to resemble one. I slipped into Britain in the early '90s, as a draft dodger with a Ph.D. in English literature. A testimony to a platonic Anglophilia which I caught in my early twenties like a mystifying virus, my undistinguished doctorate on William Hazlitt was useless even back home, let alone on board 'mother ship UK' where Ph.D.s in Eng lit are two a penny, and Hazlitt an uncool has-been amidst the fashion for post-literary study of isms and theory. I reached London as a refugee in a sea of refugees, part of a wave that was swelling in the war-torn Balkans and breaking on the hard but porous cliffs of Dover. Those who mention the lost generation when they talk of Hemingway or Fitzgerald have no idea what *lost* means.

My progress from *there* (my family's two-room flat in a concrete monstrosity on the edge of the capital, its image frozen in memory's Polaroid at the moment when the postman rang to deliver my call-up papers) to *here* (Christopher Fynch's bookshop in Chelsea on a miserable, sodden morning) involved quite a few lies, the first but not the last of which was my mother claiming that I had already escaped. It accompanied her refusal, point blank and repeated three times, like something from the Bible, to sign for anything on my behalf.

Who knew that she had it in her to decline to obey the state? She looked like a leaf the gentlest wind could blow over. She did not know that she was riddled with cancer when she drove me to the Hungarian border in the dead of the following night. Many of those who stayed on to fight later despised people like me. They called us 'runaway brides'. Mother was a better person than I. She said she would rather not see me again than see me with a gun in my hands. She had her wish.

Viewed from a distance, my path to London seems relatively painless. The parental deaths that eventually ensued and the subsequent sale of their miserable dwelling for the princely sum of ten thousand euros – the only capital I had ever possessed – only cemented my ability to disengage from feeling, a knack that was as useful as my ability to disengage from my roots. I had also and always, I admit this freely, been a lucky bastard.

After I had taken my education as far as it could formally go in order to delay the challenge and discipline of gainful employment, I found I had few ambitions. Even fewer survived the ferry crossing from Holland, where I had dossed for a couple of nights in the house of a school friend who in Belgrade was a painter of murals and in Holland had become a painter of walls. Amsterdam was full of Balkan draft dodgers high on legal weed and each other's company. Had I been in possession of any kind of manual skill I would have stayed on the mainland.

When I obtained my British work permit, I landed in book-sales just as accidentally as – before the permit became a foregone conclusion – I landed in Eaton Square, in a maisonette belonging to an American banker's British wife who wanted a male au pair for her IVF-conceived triplets. Male au pairs were fashionable. The job required no qualifications but she thought that my Ph.D.-qualified input would complement the care already provided by a full-time Filipino nanny. The Filipina was as devoted as she was inarticulate. I ferried the boys to school and took them to play football in Hyde Park. They liked me as I liked them: without attachment. When I was no longer needed as their minder, I still saw them from time to time, when they came over from Oxford, Princeton and Brown, to visit mum and dad. They read, unlike mum and dad. They dropped into the store and called me *dude* in an exaggeratedly American way. All British kids aspire to be American these days and the three boys preferred their father to their mother anyway.

I started working for Christopher Fynch in 1995. Christopher was a gentleman bookseller, in that order: a gentleman all the time and bookseller for an occasional hour or two when he bothered to turn up to check on me. He paid me miserably, but it was as much as he could afford, and often more than that. We rubbed along. He had been widowed since 1987. Although he had a stepdaughter barely younger than him somewhere in West Hampstead, he had no children of his own. He once explained that *mumps took care of that*. I doubt that he had ever been of a child-making persuasion. I am not even sure – his marriage to a woman eighteen years older than him notwithstanding – whether Christopher Fynch was homo- or heterosexual. Without being ascetic in many other ways (his daily table at La Poule au Pot and his half bottle of claret are proof of that), in matters even remotely sexual Fynch seemed to be the kind of otherworldly *old boy* for whom the concept of celibacy had been invented. He liked me, and I liked him, although I did not for a moment think that he would ever make me his heir in the book business or elsewhere. I never possessed a mercenary bone in my body – and there wasn't much to be inherited anyway.

Our enterprise remained as half-hearted as the British weather. Until the day Gorsky turned up with his piece of business. There was something so obvious in his solitary and slightly taciturn appearance that, almost from day one, I called him 'The Great Gorsky' in my e-mail exchanges with Fynch. My boss was a keen writer of e-mails in spite of his fusty Old Etonian technophobe façade. E-mails, *e-pistles* as he called them, enabled him not to get out of bed when he did not feel like it. And he was not alone. We are talking about the ageing population of an entire island in a mild stupor of post-imperial depression.

'My name is Gorsky, Roman Borisovich Gorsky,' the Prussian prince in Scottish cashmere finally said, having inspected the shelves of Christopher Fynch's for the best part of half an hour, here and there taking a volume down and leafing through it in a way that was at once careful and absent-minded. His accent was unmistakeably Russian, his English careful and correct.

'My name is Gorsky, Roman Borisovich Gorsky,' he said in a voice that mixed equal traces of softness and nicotine gravel. 'I was wondering if I might have a quick chat with you.'

'Do you speak Russian?' he asked after I stood up from my desk. A book fell off my knees and a pile of handwritten receipts scattered on the floor. I stammered something about *understanding* and *reading*. My mother tongue was similar enough.

'What do you read?' Roman Borisovich interrupted, still in English. 'From Russia, I mean.'

'Babel. Bunin. Bulgakov.'

He smiled at my row of Bs.

'But Chekhov also . . . Tolstoy, of course.' Having no idea about his literary tastes, I was trying to cover the field.

'No Dostoevsky?'

There was the merest shadow of a smirk in one corner of his upper lip. He could see I was trying to please.

'Well, yes. And no . . . I used to, once. I am not sure I would enjoy his work much now. Life is, you could say, hard enough . . .'

That sounded wrong. What was I saying about Fyodor Mikhailovich or indeed about myself? All around me there was ample evidence that life, including mine, was anything but hard. He was not paying attention anyway.

'Poetry?'

'Yes, poetry too. Tsvetaeva. Andrei Bely. Akhmatova. Blok. The Silver Age in general. And Puskhin, naturally. Like everyone else. How can you not read Pushkin?'

How profound, Nikola, I thought with deepest sarcasm, even as I reeled off my all-too-obvious list.

That, more or less, was it. *Our quick chat.* The commission that was to transform Fynch's bookshop for the best part of two years came seemingly as an afterthought. He was, already, almost out of the door when he mentioned the reason for his visit.

Gorsky was building a house down the road and we were to ensure that, on the day it was ready to occupy, it was furnished with the best library in London. The best private library in Europe. Not just any general library, but a library tailor-made for a Russian gentleman-scholar with an interest in art, literature and travel, and a flair for European languages; a library that would look as though Gorsky had acquired the books himself and read them over many years, or – if he had not already done so – was fully intending to read them. Moreover, a library that would look as though he had inherited much of its stock from bookish ancestors. Gorsky wanted first editions of everything, including the Old Testament, and he wanted his copies in mint condition.

Money was, I hardly need to add, not an issue.

'I will give you an allowance,' he said, taking a long, narrow chequebook bound in maroon crocodile skin out of his coat pocket. He paused for a couple of seconds before writing out the sum of two hundred and fifty thousand pounds, payable to *Christopher Fynch Ltd*, as a notice sellotaped to the till directed him to do. The slim barrel of his fountain pen was elaborately encrusted with pin-sized gems. The ink was dark sepia. His handwriting was both beautiful and illegible. The sum was clear enough.

'Spend the money, and when you spend it ask for more. Take thirty per cent off for your time. But I want the receipts for everything, down to the cheapest paperback. Does that seem reasonable?'

His tone suggested that he was reasonable, indeed generous, but not a fool. It suggested, moreover, that he had had some experience in dealing with people who took him for a fool and that they had found out it wasn't a good idea.

As I said, that was, more or less, it. Except, now that I think of it, for one last detail. After I had put the cheque, stupidly, fumblingly, inside the till and closed it, Gorsky gave a final little smirk and paused.

'Art books?' he asked.

'Yes. Well, no. I mean yes to Russian art, avidly so indeed, but not in Russian. Yet.' That, for a change, was absolutely true. I had spent the best part of the previous year swotting up on Russian art, reading every book I could lay my hands on, because of Natalia Summerscale.

'Good. Very good. I'd like my library to be able to enchant an art connoisseur.'

With that he walked out of the door and into the waiting car.

2

Natalia's phone call took me by surprise. Though surprise seems the faintest little word, nowhere near apt for what I felt.

'I was wondering if you have a copy of that book about Ilya Kabakov just published by Yale University Press,' she said.

I knew I was speaking to her although she hadn't introduced herself. That was the longest sentence I had ever heard her utter. Her English was softened by Russian, like forest fruit macerated in honey. Did I have that Yale book? Did I not?! I made sure we had every last title about conceptualist art, down to the rarest foreign-language chapbook appearing in places like Helsinki or Stuttgart. I had single-handedly, without Christopher Fynch even noticing it, made his bookshop the leading stockist of late Soviet art history, simply in order to keep this woman returning to us, on any book-related whim she could conceivably have. Of course we had that book. I had placed an order practically before the author had submitted his book proposal to Yale.

'Oh, I am so glad, Mr . . .' She hesitated.

'Kimović. Nikola. Nicholas, I mean. Nikola is a girl's name in English: I got bored hearing people explain that to me. Call me Nick, please.' I stumbled then paused, sensing another question in her hesitation.

'I am Serbian. You know, from Serbia. Belgrade. Not Belgravia.'

There was a mixture of relief and irony in the little peal of laughter she gave as a response. I could tell where the irony came from. I wasn't sure about the relief.

'I do know where Serbia is, Mr Kimović. Even Belgrade. I visited it as a girl with my papa. I remember a fortress where two rivers met. A big park with churches.

Outdoor cafes everywhere. What a lovely town it was.'

She offered to send someone to collect the book. She hesitated for a brief moment when I suggested I would be happy to deliver it myself. I was about to close the shop and I would welcome some fresh air and a walk. She could not be too far away, I reasoned. I heard the muffled sounds of a brief conversation then that slightly awkward laughter again.

'Yes,' she said. 'Yes. Why not?'

She spelled out the address, pausing after every letter to make sure I got it. I dutifully pretended to take the directions, and even asked a question or two, although I had known it all for months. I did not for a moment think that my errand would amount to more than the briefest exchange at the door with one of her staff, but it represented a step. Towards what, I wasn't sure. I hesitate to say it was a step forward, although it felt like one at the time.

Natalia Summerscale was one of those willowy Russian women who was so tall and so beautiful that your heart missed a beat when she entered a room. She looked like an alien princess. She looked wealthy beyond ordinary dreams of wealth. Her voice wasn't 'full of money'; she made you feel vulgar because you dared think that money had any bearing on anything. She stood out, even in this town which was full of beautiful Russian women who followed Russian money as surely as seagulls follow cruise liners. She made Grace Kelly look like a market trader. She was impossibly elegant, impossibly polite, impossibly soft spoken, and made the gentlest of movements – movements that carried a hint of some great disappointment, like someone who had spent her whole life preparing for the part of the white swan, only to lose it because she suddenly grew too tall for ballet.

I admit it. I was smitten by Natalia although I knew that she was not only married but clearly and conspicuously out of my league, and although I am not given to childish infatuation I spent hours wondering whether and when she would come into the shop. For a long while I had no idea who Mr Summerscale was. It was evident that he was not short of a penny or two. I was convinced that he must also be someone special to have been chosen by this woman, for she could have had any old billionaire she set her eyes on.

Natalia engaged in no discernible form of work beyond a vague notion of bringing a retrospective exhibition of Ilya Kabakov's art to London. That at least was what she told me when she first came through the door of Christopher Fynch's shop one February morning, wrapped in some expensive silver furs and smelling of mimosas. The car that waited for her, although superficially similar to Gorsky's, looked like the sort of thing any Saudi prince could afford. I soon learned that she did not always dress ostentatiously – in fact, she usually wore jeans and trainers – but that first appearance was almost a parody of a cinematic entrance. How could I forget it?

Over a few months thereafter, she used to turn up in the bookshop, say a polite hello, look around the art section, drop a few fifty-pound notes on the desk, name a selection of titles, then leave me to scurry around, wrap carefully and write out receipts in my most ornate longhand, adding craven thank-yous in Russian as though she was ever going to check the bills. An hour or two after she left, the driver would turn up to collect her shopping. Her library on the subject must gradually have become quite sizeable, yet weeks passed and her putative exhibition got no closer to fruition. She paid me next to no attention. I don't think she even realised that I was not English, not until that phone call many months later.

Occasionally she was accompanied by her daughter, a girl who was as blonde and willowy as the mother, and who looked as though no other genetic material was involved in her creation, as though her existence involved no conception nor labour, but parthenogenesis. The child's name was Daisy.

'You couldn't make it up,' Fynch said. 'An old Russian name, I am sure.'

I sometimes spotted Daisy in a gingham nursery dress, with a little straw boater perched on top of her head and held in place by a white elastic band under her chin, sitting in the back of the family limousine as it inched down the King's Road, its liveried driver at the wheel. She would be alone on the back seat, reading a picture book or looking out, always appearing as serene as her mother. Daisy – the name already felt too small for such an Anglo-Russian flower.

It took a while to name the feeling, so unaccustomed was I to anything like it. Could one be star-struck by someone who was not a star but something more beautiful and rare? Natalia Summerscale was a complicated Fabergé egg, a priceless object I did not desire to possess. I tried to imagine the Russian place where she might have grown up, without much success. She could have been a child prostitute or the granddaughter of Marshal Zhukov; she might have been raised in a Siberian heroin den or a lavish dacha on the outskirts of Moscow; she could have been abused by an alcoholic mother or patted on the head by some Communist walrus with bushy eyebrows and three rows of medals on his chest: no scenario made complete sense, nothing fitted her otherworldly looks. In the imagination, too, she remained out of my reach.

In those hours when I had nothing better to do – and I had more of those than most men my age – I searched the name Summerscale on the internet. I narrowed it down to a picture of a reasonably good-looking middle-aged man, a very English, strongly built man, like a former army officer, or someone who played rugby rather than cricket at school, but neither long nor well enough to have had his nose broken. He was wearing a dinner jacket over a full, broad chest, and coming out of some charity bash at Claridge's. Natalia hung on his arm like a silk kite about to take off.

Mr and Mrs Thomas Summerscale, the caption read. They had paid fifteen thousand pounds at an auction for a dinner with Jeremy Paxman or someone similar. For child leukaemia. No mention of what he did for a living, let alone of what she might be doing.

I dropped Summerscale's name into conversations with my Brookner readers and even one or two of my e-mails to Fynch and I got contradictory responses.

They live in that old hospital off Fulham Road, said one lady. Spent over two years doing it up, drilling God alone knows how deep into the London soil. There was a rumour that she had a slide, a spiral chrome tube, descending two storeys from her bedroom to her private swimming pool in the basement. Also a Russian steam room lined with pre-Raphaelite mosaics assembled from semi-precious stones. Like Kubla Khan's palace in Xanadu. And the largest private garden in Chelsea.

Old money, said another.

Far too much money being splashed around to be old, said the third.

No one seemed to know what Summerscale was doing in London now, but most suspected he acted as a kind of consigliere for the Russians. The English liked to say that talking about money was vulgar yet they talked about little else. In fact, only earning it appeared to trouble them; spending it, especially on property, was definitely not a taboo.

'I knew his father, something or other in the British embassy in Moscow after the war,' said Fynch. 'Good old Cold War days. Decent chap. Young Thomas Summerscale was called to the bar in the late eighties, went over to Moscow with an American consultancy, hooked up with a few people his father knew, came back with trainloads of Russian money and that stunning Russian wife. Had an English wife before. Somewhere in Gloucestershire.'

He knew Summerscale's father-in-law too. The first one. A vicar, apparently. A bit on the high side, so a Father. Birettas, bambini, that sort of thing, but nonetheless of the marrying kind. He trailed off into one of his C of E tirades, which usually ended with him wondering how each Archbishop of Canterbury managed to be worse than his predecessor. The Russians held no interest for him unless they were opera singers.

The address of the hospital was still on a creaking NHS website, illustrated with old pictures – a Gothic folly with a ramp for disabled patients stretching like a drawbridge across a moat, and dozens of blue and white signs for the now redundant wards, their names telling a PC version of British history. No Drakes. No Nelsons. No Nightingales even. Edna this and Frank that. Mainly Ednas.

I knew the building well. I had walked the streets around it many times, looking over the high walls, across the regimentally striped lawns, trying to see through the ranks of espaliered trees into the darkened windows. The place was called The Laurels, after the hospice that still stood in one corner of the grounds but now looked as though it might house staff accommodation. I never saw anyone coming in or out of The Laurels' richly lacquered double front doors. The house must have underground access, I thought, or some kind of tradesman's entrance hidden from view. How could I guess the way these places worked?

The edifice was so large it could have contained a whole other house inside, a cosier place, like those quaint little mock-cottages at Versailles or Potsdam in which the royals played happy middle-class families; where Natalia and Thomas Summerscale could sit of an evening and watch their daughter practise on her piano while the servants glided along the corridors of the big house, bringing martinis, or camomile tea. A cosy little cottage with a study where Natalia leafed through her expensive editions of conceptualist monographs, planning her great exhibition. It was difficult to see what her planning might involve and why she even bothered dreaming of an event like that. I tried to picture her in the warm glow of a reading lamp, perhaps wearing a pair of tortoiseshell spectacles, but fantasising about her day-to-day life was a bit like dreaming of a hand-crafted yacht. I had none of the components needed to put the dream together.

I spied Natalia on the lawn in front of The Laurels only once. She was holding the arm of Daisy who in turn was holding a tennis racket. They were accompanied by someone who seemed familiar from Wimbledon. They were rehearsing a backhand. I glimpsed them from the top of a double-decker bus and I turned away before either of them could have spotted me. By then I was already living practically across the road, a bit closer to the river, in the gatekeeper's cottage of a property whose main building was so majestic that it towered over The Laurels. It was a baroque edifice that had once housed an army barracks, with a central dome as big as a cathedral's and miles of covered colonnades. It looked too grand for a ministry, imposing enough perhaps for the parliament of a medium-sized country.

It had been surrounded for months by tall hoardings while it underwent a process of reconstruction that in its elaborateness seemed to dwarf anything that the

Summerscales had done: less like a private enterprise and more like the rebuilding of the Old Royal Naval College at Greenwich, or St Paul's Cathedral. Even the hoardings around the construction site were painted in an expensive shade of primrose yellow, with the name of a famous architectural practice superimposed on them in midnight-blue in an elegant font. It was the sort of outfit you might engage to add an extra wing to the Louvre or construct a new bridge across the Thames.

I lived in the shadow of the project for a few months whilst having no idea if the new owner was ever going to show up. This stretch of Chelsea by the river was money-central, a weird corner of a weird city. The rent on my little cottage – it was a mere matchbox, one room stacked above another – amounted to practically nothing because I was happy to live next to the building site for as long as the building took, and happy to confirm that I would leave with a month's notice as soon as the build was completed. The previous occupant of the cottage had left after the freeholder bribed him in order to sell the place to the Big House. The vast structure that overshadowed my home was officially listed as the Chelsea Yeomanry Barracks, although that certainly wasn't what the place was going to be called. It was too grand to be a villa, too magnificent to need a name. It made Buckingham Palace look like an ungainly box by a roundabout.

Even the machinery on the site seemed more suited to large-scale surface mining than domestic architecture. The digging was so extensive that my cottage rattled and hummed with the vibrations. Its walls cracked like the shell of an egg dropped from a great height. New fissures stretched like cobwebs across every wall. I watched from the upstairs windows as Caterpillar trucks criss-crossed fields of freshly dug earth, the smell of which filled my bedroom and permeated my clothes. Armies of junior architects in white safety helmets and yellow high-visibility jackets marched around, builders shouted at each other in Polish all day, cranes as tall as Nelson's Column went up and down. The entire colossal edifice was being dismantled in order for it to be rebuilt. Enormous mature trees were wrenched up and moved from one place to another to create the sort of avenue Haussmann was fond of in Paris but which the English only ever attempt in the open countryside, well away from their capital, in places where no one but sheep can admire it.

At one point nothing remained but a wall of honeyed stone with tall elegant windows and, behind it, heavy metal girders supporting the dome under which, further beyond, you could glimpse the Thames in its languid flow. It seemed as though I was witnessing the building of the Tower of Babel, turned upside down in obeisance to British planning laws, and plunging into the flaming heart of our planet.

I soon got used to the tremors that shook my new dwelling. I took to fragmentation like a fish to water: contingency was my element, my natural habitat. I wondered what, if anything, Natalia could feel across two lanes of traffic and the two hundred yards of her front garden, inside her cottage-within-a-castle set-up, if that's what it was. There was no amount of money that could keep things as quiet for anyone in London as successfully as having no money at all. There must be whole squares in the few still unfashionable parts of the East End that have seen no building work in two decades, not even a lick of paint. But everywhere around here the drilling, the digging and the movements of men, machinery and materials were never-ending.

Had she wanted peace and quiet, I reasoned, she would not have settled in Chelsea. She would have purchased, if not a stately home, then some former general's or MP's house tucked away in Hampshire or Dorset, a place with its own trout stream. British generals and parliamentarians no longer had the sort of capital needed to keep the trout swimming. It was easy to get hold of a quiet abode if you kept ten million in your current account.

I locked the bookshop promptly at five and walked through squares of tall Victorian mansion blocks and down the King's Road with a parcel under my arm. I was in a daze, rehearsing possible variants of short speeches, in case Natalia opened the door in person. I was keen to make an impression although I wasn't sure about its purpose. I wasn't even sure I wanted to know more than the sketchiest nothings which fuelled my thoughts of her.

Her Russianness did not affect me in the way Russianness seems to affect British men, with that undercurrent of sexual thrill that was there even when they weren't sure whether to cast these East European beauties as submissive pre-feminist goddesses, designed – and designing themselves – purely to please men, or as scary Amazons from James Bond movies ready to exploit your every weakness, each one an impossible cross between Lara Croft and Felix Dzerzhinsky. And although I found it fascinating, Natalia's wealth wasn't in itself attractive. There seemed to be just too much of it; it was the kind of money that not only begets money but demands its own space, its own share of your life. It was the kind of money that takes over and becomes a full-time occupation.

The kind of wealth I envied was the getting-by sort, the Christopher Fynch sort, the equivalent of a couple of hundred thousand pounds somehow forever topping itself up in your deposit account even as you eat your *steak au poivre* and drink your claret; the sort of money that cascaded down the generations and seeped through ramshackle businesses and holes in moth-eaten dinner jackets until everyone forgot where it came from; the sort of money that wasn't even affluence so much as a sense of entitlement. I had always known that there were millionaires and billionaires, but Fynch's capital was the sort of wealth I'd never known existed until I came to England.

My mother, a school teacher and the family treasurer, divided banknotes into six envelopes on the first of every month when my parents received their salaries in cash: standing charges, food, clothing, pocket money, holidays and savings. Everything that remained unspent in the first five envelopes on the last day of the month went into that final one, to translate eventually into a washing machine or a TV set, or to be put aside for a rainy day. These came with inevitable regularity: things broke down, wore out, died.

Christopher Fynch's money gave you choices without obligations. I couldn't see why someone like Thomas Summerscale would even want to make the leap from the world of that money – the sort of money his old-school diplomat father would doubtless have possessed – to the world he now moved in. Was it his greed to possess women like Natalia, or did it originate in a drive stronger than that – boredom with the Christopher Fynches and their England, a desire to ride with the global big boys? Or simply circumstance? Finding himself in Russia in the early 1990s, with all that cash floating about amid so much poverty, must have done strange things to men like Summerscale. How does a respectable English barrister become a carpetbagger, a court advisor to the new tsars? What does such a transformation do to a man's mind?

The bell echoed down some endless corridor as I stood between two CCTV cameras which pointed at the top of my head while I tried discreetly to wipe my feet on a thick doormat flanked by carefully trimmed bay trees in huge black pots carved from what looked like obsidian. By the time I reached The Laurels the rain had seeped into my shoes and was creeping up my socks. I wasn't sure whether I'd be invited in and, if I were granted entry, was even less sure what kind of etiquette the Summerscale household observed. When I worked as au pair, my 'house mother' insisted on people taking their shoes off inside the front door and walking barefoot across the marble floors. Everything in that household was 'bohemian' in a neurotic, controlling kind of way, so casual it allowed no dissent. Natalia could not possibly be like that. She did not seem like a woman who would notice whether a man was wearing shoes, or deign to worry about wet socks.

I imagined acres of white Bukhara carpets ahead of me and the imprints my feet might leave on them. I could, perhaps, drop the parcel and run. Or would they, if I did so, replay the film from their CCTV and point, laughing, inviting Daisy to join in? There was no way to get out now. Like the clerk Yepikhodov and his squeaking boots, my wet feet and I seemed destined to play bit parts in the Summerscale rendition of *The Cherry Orchard*.

As I waited for the door to open and listened out for footsteps, conjuring different possibilities, I never expected to see Thomas Summerscale in front of me. He materialised, barefoot, wearing an old Aran jumper and a pair of threadbare red corduroy trousers. He pushed a mop of hair off his face before he offered his hand in a handshake.

'Good evening, Nicholas. I am Tom. Tom Summerscale. Please come in. Natalia told me to expect you,' he said, somehow implying by his expression that she had told him much more than that, that he thought she and I were friends.

He clearly did not expect me to take off my shoes although I wasn't too far off on the white silk Bukhara. The softest, whitest pile imaginable stretched ahead of me. Behind the double front door, it covered acres of the vast lobby, lit by a huge chandelier suspended from the high ceiling and constructed of strangely twisted glass, like a teeming nest of translucent serpents. It was a near twin – almost as big – of the Chihuly chandelier in the lobby of the V&A. Pieces of artwork dotted the cavernous space. It was soundproofed so well that I could hear my own heartbeat. Around us stood several lifesize classical statues in white marble, their broken fingers pointing at the ceiling or the door. One held a couple of scarves across its sole surviving arm. The head of another was half obscured by a small straw boater with a blue grosgrain ribbon.

Summerscale stood there and smiled, allowing me moments to take it all in. He was clearly used to his visitors' double-take, though he did not look like someone who had much interest in any of the pieces around us. He made no effort to explain what they were, although I hardly managed to hide my curiosity.

On one wall hung an enormous black canvas overlaid with smaller squares in different shades of black. Against the opposite wall, propped on the floor rather than hung, was an equally huge framed monochrome photograph of a toothless man leering into the camera. He stood in the middle of what looked like the bleakest of Communist marketplaces. Rows of empty stands roofed with rusting corrugated metal sheeting and dusted with scraps of dirty snow stretched behind him. I did not notice, until I had almost passed the image, that the man's penis hung out of his open flies. It was shrivelled but enormous nonetheless, the most obscenely sized detumescent male organ imaginable. The thought that Daisy had to walk past it every day seemed even more gross than the photograph itself.

'Russians, eh!' Summerscale laughed at my effort to pretend I wasn't shocked, and slapped me on the back as if to encourage me to speed up. It was only then that I saw that he was carrying, under his left arm, a copy of Antony Beevor's *Stalingrad*. It was one of those thick history books Fynch could never afford to run out of: a 'steady seller', in our corner of London, for people who needed to spice their prosperous and comfortable lives with tales of horror and desperation that bore the hallmark of history, rather than mere entertainment. There was something of Antony Beevor about Tom Summerscale's appearance too, although Summerscale was both more muscular and more caddish.

'Are you enjoying that?' I nodded towards the volume. An embroidered bookmark stuck out between its pages about two thirds of the way through.

'The Russians,' he repeated, this time with a shrug and without making any effort to respond to my question. He was now taking me through another double doorway and blocking my view into the room as he turned towards me. I was, at five foot eight, a good five inches shorter than him, and I weighed probably a third less.

'You can't defeat them unless they wish to be defeated. They are like beasts. They will die in their millions, without needing the consolations of an afterlife. You'll never find such men and women anywhere else. Forget about the Muslims. They blow themselves up in the hope of seventy-two cherries to pop. The Russians are scarier. They fight hoping for nothing. Do you know Natalia is from Stalingrad? Volgograd as it was called by the time she was born. Daddy was a Stalingrad rat, fifteen in 1945. It takes a special kind of zest to survive all that and then procreate so unstoppably. He had five children in a country in which most people stop at two. And not even religious. Unless you count Communism . . .'

Summerscale sighed as though a zest for life was not altogether a praiseworthy trait and turned sideways to let me through. At the far end of the drawing room, there was Natalia, in a dress so simple it could have been a taller girl's version of her daughter's school uniform. She was sitting on a blindingly white sofa, holding the hands of another woman and smiling at me in welcome as though nothing in her husband's speech related to her or as though she had not heard any of it. She made no effort to explain to Summerscale that there was no way I could have known where she was born, that I was neither her cousin nor her friend, that I was barely even an acquaintance.

'Let me relieve you of that,' Summerscale said with a faint snigger. He took the book parcel from me and handed it to a maid who was standing to attention a couple of feet away. She held it in both hands like a salver and continued to stand on the same spot, awaiting orders.

The woman next to Natalia looked extraordinary. She seemed considerably shorter – although not short herself – and she wore a tight red jersey dress, like a V-neck jumper, which ended just above her knees. Underneath it, her body seemed constructed from a bundle of thick ropes tied tightly against each other, all muscle and bone and artificially tanned skin. Her collarbones jutted out to such a degree that a pendant she wore on a thin gold chain around her neck almost disappeared behind them. Her small pert breasts looked as though they were made of muscle and not of fat deposits. It was obvious that she was wearing no bra, but also that she did not need one. Her erect nipples showed through like buttons on shirt pockets.

I am talking about this woman's body because I have no idea of how to begin to describe her face. It was uncannily familiar, somehow youthful but older than it should be – like those computer simulations that artificially age a young face. Her skin was that of a windsurfer, not so much wrinkled as damaged by exposure to sun, but it clung tightly to her high cheekbones: it seemed as though her skull was coming through. Yet she was bubbling with energy and somehow handsome with it all.

'Gergana Pekarova,' Natalia said and released Gergana's hands. Pekarova jumped to her feet and grasped both of my hands simultaneously. Her handshake – left- and right-handed alike – was firmer than Tom Summerscale's and that is saying something.

'Gery is a famous Bulgarian gymnast, an Olympic gold

medallist,' Summerscale added as he disappeared off into the bowels of the house.

'She is my personal trainer. And my daughter's . . .' Natalia explained. She showed no intention to stand up or shake my hand.

'And art advisor,' Pekarova said with a faintest smile. You did not know whether she was joking or not. She looked sophisticated enough to make the claim plausible.

She led me to an armchair which faced the sofa at an angle. The leather the chair was made of, like the sofa, was covered in tiny bumps. I wondered what creature – or more likely hundreds of them – was sacrificed to create these items. My urge to stroke the arms of the chair was only marginally weaker than the fear of leaving my fingerprints all over. Some poor soul was likely to be dealing with my wet footprints in the lobby at that very moment.

Natalia nodded at the servant who unwrapped the parcel, deposited the book on an embroidered footstool, folded the wrapping paper into a neat square, then waited again.

'Please let Boyana and Maria know that we are ready,' Gergana Pekarova said and dismissed the woman.

Natalia smiled at me and thanked me for the book, barely glancing at it.

Behind the sofa stood a glass pillar encasing an amazing scene: snowflakes falling on a statue of a naked man. His figure was a couple of feet tall and apparently made of frozen blood. His empty sockets stared towards me like the eyes of a monstrous aborted foetus.

Two maids wheeled in an enormous silver samovar. I stood up to leave but Natalia touched my arm.

'Stay,' she said. She spoke softly, yet uttered an order nonetheless. It was a tone one might use to housetrain a Pomeranian puppy. I felt my face spread into a smile, the likeness of which I had not attempted since I left my socialist kindergarten.

Gery Pekarova thanked the women in Bulgarian and started busying herself with platefuls of pastries and sandwiches, all the while asking questions about Fynch's bookshop and me, about both of which she was, apparently, well informed. Did I enjoy my work, do people read nowadays, what sort of books, how do we decide what to stock among the thousands of titles published every year? While I fielded the barrage of questions, Natalia listened, silent.

When, in turn, I asked Pekarova about her life behind the Iron Curtain and her successes as a gymnast, she responded half-heartedly – not so much evasively but as though the topic bored her. Natalia turned away from me, looked into the eyes of the bloody foetus behind her, and sighed.

'Let us not talk about Communism,' she said. 'It is so boring. You sound so English, Mr Kimović. What Iron Curtain? I have never seen it. Have you? Let us talk of art, of beautiful things.'

I did not dare say that her art collection, judging by what was on show inside The Laurels, hardly inspired talk of beautiful things. Yet her eyes – and Gery's – lit up when I obeyed and started praising the pieces on display everywhere around us. I recognised broad trends; I guessed at names; I faked enthusiasm. Gery put a price tag on every piece, each amounting to more than the price of a small house, even in this corner of the city. And every time Gery mentioned a sum, Natalia rolled her eyes slightly – as if to indicate that she disagreed with such a display of vulgar instincts – yet she did not stop her. Natalia clearly knew the market much better than I would have given her credit for, and she did not collect only the Russians. There were the Young Brits, the Spaniards and the French, even a piece by a Vietnamese installation artist based in Zurich, a sewing machine twisted to look like a racehorse.

It was a matter of huge sorrow, the women agreed, that they did not manage to secure Tracey Emin's tent, although they bid hundreds of thousands of pounds for it. Had it been at The Laurels, Gery said, it would not have perished in the fire.

I had a vague memory of a blaze that destroyed a number of artworks in a warehouse in East London some years previously. I was taken aback by the passion with which they spoke of Emin, referring to the artist by her first name and with the warmth normally reserved for friends or family members.

'I'd have given Tracey a whole room,' Natalia sighed, 'I admire her work so much. I'd have put it on a green Bessarabian kilim, against my favourite Chinese wallpaper with cherry trees, to make it look real. What do you think, Gery? Like a camping site in Kent, in Margate, no?'

She pronounced the name as though it was French – *Ma-gatte* – in a way that did not suggest that she was more than abstractly familiar with England. That the three of us should have converged on London from our different corners of Eastern Europe to sit on dodo or basilisk skin and eat macaroons while discussing Tracey Emin's embroidery felt more than surreal. I had rehearsed Russian and Soviet art stories on the way there, hoping to impress Natalia, yet the only time she displayed a glimmer of curiosity about me was when, on our third porcelain cup of Oolong tea, Pekarova and I started discussing Serbian tennis.

'Djoković,' said the Bulgarian, 'your compatriot, no? A handsome boy. Sexy.'

Natalia suddenly stood up and took us both by the hand.

'I have a great idea, Gery. Why don't you and Mr Kimović take my tickets for the Wimbledon finals this year? I am sick of corporate hospitality. All those friends of Tom's trying to be entertaining. And I don't even think that strawberries and champagne go together. The English have the palates of small boys.'

She placed Gery's hand over mine and held them thus. The Bulgarian threw an extraordinary smile in my direction. Her tanned cheeks sank under her cheekbones while her lips, covered by a thick layer of red lipstick, plumped up over her improbably white teeth. She looked like a female – or not so female – version of Mick Jagger, yet I had to admit that, although outlandish, she was far from unattractive. Her fine long legs and her long neck gave her the appearance of a thoroughbred Arabian horse. Without Natalia to compare her to, I would even have called her sexy.

I sensed myself blushing to the roots of my hair. This was clearly matchmaking, yet there was something vaguely humiliating about the exercise. Was Natalia Summerscale putting me in my place by linking me, however tentatively, with her personal trainer?

Daisy arrived carrying a folder of music sheets. Natalia stood up and held Daisy's head in both hands to plant a wordless kiss on her blonde parting. The child barely glanced at the rainbow-coloured stacks of macaroons piled high around the samovar and took none. She whispered good evening and continued on her way. I used the interruption as a cue to offer my apologies and leave.

No one would have called the visit a success, but it could have been much worse. On the way home, I made a huge loop around The Laurels, cutting through The Boltons, as though I was trying to cover my tracks. Victorian crescents glistened. The sound of car wheels on gravel driveways punctuated the steady hum of rain. The rich interiors, with their carefully draped curtains and flower arrangements, seemed open to the world and positively cosy compared to The Laurels. I could imagine people collapsing into deep velvet sofas at the end of their evening, checking their e-mails, doing the crossword, listening to music. These were the lives I could still, just about, make some sense of.

An hour later, I was almost back where I started. I bought a cup of coffee on the ground floor of the Chelsea and Westminster Hospital, in whose huge atrium I sat for a couple of hours watching patients and medical staff riding up and down escalators. High above us all, rain pattered against the panes of the glass roof. There was a flower shop behind the cafe and, next to it, several tables stacked with books donated to a cancer charity.

Please help yourself and leave as much as you can, said a note attached to a green collecting jar. I emptied my wallet into it – a tenner and a few loose coins. There was no book I wanted.

In a Serbian hospital a visitor wouldn't have made it past the porter at this late hour. Here, everything was open, even to a casual visitor like me who had no business inside. The British are squeamish about death, but they have no problem with sickness, so long as we are talking about the body rather than the soul. The body can bend to the will of the soul. You might be born male but become a woman, you can tattoo and pierce your skin, change the colour of your hair and the shape of your teeth and your nose, you can enlarge or reduce your breasts, adjust your outward appearance to whatever you want it to be. The only thing you are not allowed to be is unhappy, particularly if you are an immigrant. Unhappiness is a form of ingratitude, an abuse of hospitality.

In the course of our surreal tea party, Natalia Summerscale had stood up from her sofa twice: once to take Gery Pekarova's hands and link them with mine, once to kiss the top of her daughter's head. And both times she held my gaze and said: 'I am so happy. So, so happy.'

I did not believe it for a moment.

The rain was soft and steady. When I returned home, one of the gates to the building site next door was ajar. Curious to see the works, I walked in and found myself in the middle of a landscape that looked like a First World War battlefield. I carried on along the improvised walkway that stretched over mounds of freshly dug earth. The Thames glimmered faintly through the trees. A solitary barge glided eastwards towards the City and its money mills, and further onwards to Docklands where, amid the towering offices, warehouses that once stored spice and sugar from the colonies were now echoing minimalist apartments and shiny, antiseptic gyms with treadmills and rowing machines powered by the energy of finance. The enormous statue of Buddha on the northern edge of Battersea Park surveyed from the south bank the scene of desolation across the river. High above me, the baroque dome, suspended on a vast iron grid, offered some protection from the rain, like a stone umbrella.

I turned away from the river to light a cigarette and realised that in doing so I had gained a direct line of sight – at some distance – into the upper floors of The Laurels. The complicated shapes of its extraordinary chandeliers sparkled behind the fine muslin curtains, but the cavernous rooms they illuminated seemed completely empty.

I heard a muffled cough and realised that someone was standing right beside me, leaning against one of the stone columns that, for the moment, supported nothing. I turned towards the sound and immediately recognised the long face and the distinctive hair, which seemed moonlit even in daytime. The evening light made it look like liquid silver.

'You know, young man, you shouldn't trespass like this. Didn't you see the warning? *Hard hats must be worn.* And it is usually alarmed around here. At least no one can accuse you of wanting to steal a Corinthian column.'

'I live just over the wall.' I nodded towards my little cottage.

'We are next-door neighbours then. Or soon will be. But not for long, perhaps. I am sure you know. I will need to put a roof over my boys' heads.' He flicked his hand as if to dismiss me, but as he did so, I noticed three men in black leather jackets further around the colonnade step back into darkness.

I bade Gorsky goodnight and descended along the makeshift pathway. The windows of the house opposite disappeared behind the tall hedges. I heard the striking of a match and further away, where Gorsky's men stood, the panting of dogs tugging on their leashes.

3

In London, April is not the cruellest month but the gentlest. No other season compares to those occasional crisp sunny days which arrive after months of slushy semifreddo, that icy drizzle that never becomes snow, never latches on. You almost forget that the sun is still somewhere out there, above the dirty duvet of cloud that covers the city as though it were a depressed patient unwilling to step out of bed. Suddenly the light breaks through and teases out every bit of red around. You realise that the place is defined by its scarlets and its blacks: red for the post boxes and phone booths, the buses, the coats of Chelsea Pensioners and the guards on duty in front of the royal palaces; black for the taxis, the heavy doors, gates and railings, for iron enclosures everywhere.

Then, as though prompted by an invisible Pied Piper, the milky green grass emerges and amidst it flowers in every colour, like light refracted through a prism. One remembers that no other city in the world has so many parks, so many gardens. The million-pound handkerchief-sized lawns join up into one continuous floral ribbon trailing from Green Park all the way to Richmond and Hampton Court – a relay race of hellebores, daffodils, hyacinths and crocuses under the parasols of magnolia and cherry blossom. In no other city can it be so good to be a bee.

The sap rises. At night, you hear urban foxes, yowling like abandoned babies, the click-clack of high heels on pavements, the ringing of mobile phones and voices saturated with boozy laughter and desire.

Next door, building work continued ceaselessly. Under spotlights that would have put a football stadium to shame, huge forks crunched the gritty under-soil, earthmovers shifted tons of wet dirt. At dawn, before the builders arrived, gulls hovered and screamed over skips full of rubble. I imagined them to be fellow stowaways from the grey expanses of the northern seas which connect the marshy estuaries of the Thames and the Neva, and the two imperial cities between which Gorsky's money flowed in a gilded cascade. He must have continued to turn up occasionally, but I did not see him again for weeks, although he was now my employer just as effectively as he was the employer of the platoons of builders whose bare muscles shone under their sleeveless high-visibility vests. He gave me the best job of my life.

I once dreamed of being a writer but found that I was too lazy to put words on paper. Now I was determined to make Gorsky's library my literary masterpiece, a work of fiction as imaginative as any story composed of words, a piece of installation art rivalling anything Natalia wanted to showcase. Every volume in Gorsky's library would connect with every other one and create a perfect text: the collection would be a work of characterisation as perfect as that of Julien Sorel or Ivan Karamazov. When he briefed me about my task, Gorsky spoke about it enchanting an art connoisseur. I aimed to accomplish more. I wanted to imagine a woman falling in love with him simply by walking through his library; that love too would be my creation.

I had little experience of antiquarian book sales but Gorsky's commission was far too big to be achieved with new stock alone. It required both the present and the past. I scoured auction catalogues for the rarest books and manuscripts, even ancient scrolls. I forwarded lists of purchases and I gradually lost count of the number of top-up cheques I received: the first edition of *Childe Harold* dedicated by Byron to Mary Shelley, Pushkin's personal bible, Thomas Macaulay's *History of England* with the stamp of the school library at Harrow and exam annotations by a fourteen-year-old Winston Churchill, *Seasons in Hell* bound in leather reclaimed from a valise Rimbaud purchased in Luxor – the original address tag with his handwriting refashioned into a bookmark. There were Renaissance quartos stitched by the best Venetian bookbinders and rare copies of German novels saved from Nazi pyres, their charred edges still smelling faintly of ashes. Then there were the latest glossy volumes with high-resolution photographs which I purchased purely to indulge Natalia Summerscale, should she ever set foot in her neighbour's library. My collection – Gorsky's collection – was taking shape in its expensive, humidity-controlled storage facility as it awaited the day when the shelves, still to be constructed out of acres of rare wood, were ready to carry it in its full magnificence.

I occasionally allowed myself the indulgence of taking one of those precious volumes home, or leafing through it at my desk at Fynch's, hoping that Natalia would turn up and catch me at it. Here and there, I cut the pages with Fynch's yellowing ivory paperknife. I did not feel I was transgressing. I doubted if many of them would ever be read otherwise, and it would have been a sin if objects as beautiful as these were not to be adored even once.

Sometimes, late at night, while the floodlights from next door streamed through chinks in my drawn curtains, I thought of moving out of the area and closer to 'my kind'.

I was never sure what that would mean. My co-nationals gathered in 'our' church in Notting Hill or in a handful of cafes in Acton and Ealing where they talked of politics and defeat. If I belonged anywhere, it was, vaguely, among the uprooted bohemian types eking out a living in jobs similar to mine, a kind of protracted adolescence possible only in a city where no one knows you and you don't care about anyone's judgement. They were as likely to be English as Japanese or Armenian, but they obsessed about their espressos more than about their nationality. They shared ramshackle homes in places like Walthamstow or Peckham, where the main streets were lined with African markets, fried chicken vendors and laptop repair shops, but, unlike here in Chelski, the realm of extreme wealth, they frequented cafes where people sat and talked without looking around for better or more important company, and visited parks where young families came out to play on Saturday afternoons in the same clothes they had been wearing since they got up. Their houses and flats were lived in, their pavements walked upon. Children's voices competed with birdsong. The deserted streets around my home were like cemeteries lined with gleaming monuments to money: silent, heavily secured sepulchres for people who were buried in the work of wealth creation.

I had no friends and I wasn't looking for a soulmate, although I was not a younger version of my sexless boss. There were enough women in London who preferred to lead their intimate lives in short and uncomplicated bursts. With no strings attached, they call it. It was possible to find sex on those terms whenever you wanted it, and without having to pay. And you didn't even have to be particularly handsome. There is a cruel freedom about this city, the freedom of an entire world on the make.

I usually banished my thoughts of relocating by early morning, when I set off on my regular jog along the Thames, alongside the long-distance buses coming into Victoria Coach Station with their cargoes of bleary-eyed East Europeans waking up from the transcontinental ride into London's new reality, a bustling market for human labour where they will become bricklayers and plumbers, nannies and waitresses, and reinvent the fundamental principles of their being in the process. I may have looked like an image of the bright new world to them, this strange new place in which men and women had so little to do that they pounded the pavements early in the morning, clutching plastic bottles in their hands, but I was just a cuckoo spotting fellow cuckoos. I ran back towards the moneyed Chelsea nest that I had usurped with so little effort, past my first employer's home in Eaton Square and past Christopher Fynch's shop, which I would open in an hour or two. It looked so inviting and timeless with its teetering piles of books leaning against the windows and its announcements of local pottery classes and small-time classical music concerts in church halls. I often paused in one of the cafes around Sloane Square and watched the early-morning arrivals pouring out of the underground station: sales staff about to open the stores, professional dog walkers on their way up to Hyde Park with half a dozen empty leashes in each hand, au pairs and nannies hurrying to take their uniformed charges to local schools, waiters and cooks, hairdressers, beauticians, manicurists and pedicurists, acupuncturists, masseurs, life coaches and psychotherapists, personal assistants, psychic healers and spiritual guides, professional de-clutterers, hundreds and hundreds of people like me offering every form of personal service imaginable.

Easter came late. It was almost May, and one of those rare years when both the Eastern Orthodox and the Catholic holiday fell on the same day as the Passover. The bookshop was going to stay open, but Christopher Fynch suddenly declared that I must take a day off. I hadn't had a Sunday off in ten years, he argued, and he was having his mother over. He needed some time away from her or he would go mad. 'Mater' was ancient enough to remember sharing a dance teacher with Daphne du Maurier's younger sister Bing in her – and Bing's – teens, but was still as sharp as a razor. When she telephoned the shop to 'check on Christopher', she spoke about him as though I was his house matron, or – as his school would have it – his dame.

I did not feel like taking a day off. There was no one and nothing I wanted to see and I hardly wanted to stay at home reading books when I could do that more comfortably at work, with fewer distractions. Now I had nothing better to do than join a procession of worshippers somewhere for a bit of people watching, choral music and incense-fumed aromatherapy.

I did not expect to see Natalia Summerscale at Ennismore Gardens, even if she turned up. Easter is the main holiday in the Orthodox calendar in every sense, not just in the narrow theological one of the Christmas-dominated West, and the Russian church gets so packed that the congregation spills out into the surrounding streets. There are hundreds of families with children carrying baskets of elaborately painted eggs, or bringing their Kulich cakes for a blessing on trays held high in front of them. Every variant of Russia abroad is normally to be seen there: from the patrician old guard to the Soviet colonials who had arrived much more recently from places like Kazakh- or other stans; from the impoverished Russian-Lithuanians on their EU passports who now clean the London streets, to the globe-trotting billionaires with wads of fifty-pound notes, which they deposit with a flourish when the collection tray comes around.

*

I did not expect to see Natalia and I assumed Gorsky wouldn't be there either. If he believed in God at all, I suspected that he worshipped in a different kind of temple. The truth, when it emerged, was to shape our final encounter.

I was about to take the last corner before the familiar Romanesque portico of the former Anglican place of worship when I spotted Natalia and Gery just ahead, holding Daisy's hands. All three wore white. With her hair gathered in a long plait, Daisy looked like a tiny version of the Russian fairy tale's Vassilisa the Beautiful. Gery carried a large basket of eggs painted in red, gold and silver. When they turned into the church, I walked straight ahead and across Hyde Park and Bayswater, past the Greek cathedral with its own Easter worshippers, and then up Portobello Road, alongside the tourists hunting for antique bargains and famous film locations.

In a quiet side street, the Serbian church was full of new British Serbs, the preceding decade's refugees from the wars in Bosnia and Croatia, standing in tight groups and waiting to receive communion after the forty days of Lent. This was still a blue-collar world. There were no billionaires here. Flocks of mournful frescoed angels were taking off into rafters blackened by decades of smoke and incense. A large crack in one of the sidewalls zigzagged like a trail left by lightning.

For a long moment after we collided, and as we both apologised, I did not recognise him. He was wearing a hideous blue tracksuit and a black beanie hat pulled low over his forehead. He looked like someone in the midst of a strenuous jog, but it was an odd corner of London to be jogging in if you lived in Chelsea. We were in one of the side streets between Golborne Road and the Westway flyover, just behind the Serbian church, one of the many indistinguishable Victorian terraces that housed Caribbean immigrants in the 1950s, then the Spanish and Portuguese labourers from what were then impoverished Iberian dictatorships, and finally a wave of North Africans escaping Maghrebian politics and the grimness of French satellite towns. On any weekend, men in loose djellabas and babouches sat in front of working men's cafes sipping mint tea and smoking. The market looked like a street scene in Fez or Algiers.

Tom Summerscale laughed, unfazed. He had taken notice of me perhaps only because of the look of astonishment on my face.

'I am just stopping for some oysters and Porter around the corner. Why not join me?' he said, as though there was nothing unusual about the situation; as though we had, in fact, arranged to meet.

I joined him out of curiosity. Something told me that – like me – he was not a man with many friends. We took a table in one of those gentrified pubs that had become so common in the area: places that looked like a film version of 1947. Fake austerity permeated every detail of the *mise-en-scène*, every hook on the wall and every plate and glass. The beer was as black as coal, the butter was almost yellow, the bread so warm it was smoking, and the oysters were still alive.

We made odd dining companions. I was wearing what passes for my Sunday best. He was dressed like a roofer on his way home from a day's shift, but gaggles of Notting

Hill girls drinking their first cocktails of the day looked at him rather than me. His public school ruddiness and his posh baritone were impossible to disguise.

I half listened to his insights into Russian politics, told for the benefit of surrounding tables rather than for mine, becoming alert only when Natalia's name was mentioned. This part of his ramblings, although much quieter, was worth paying attention to because he was surprisingly frank. They had been married for just over seven years. Natalia had abandoned her studies of art history in St Petersburg to come to Britain with him. Summerscale was urging her to continue. She was, it seems, reluctant. He was offering to open a small gallery to keep her entertained. She would get very enthusiastic, then relent. She used to be so full of energy when he first knew her, so unafraid. It was as though all she had ever wanted was to go West, he said, but now that she was here, she couldn't quite figure out who she was supposed to be.

It felt as though he was asking for some piece of advice I couldn't give. We sat in silence for a while.

'I have an appointment, Nick, old boy.' Summerscale eventually looked at his watch. 'Why don't you come with me? I'll drive you back afterwards. It will only take a minute and you'll enjoy seeing old Mahdi.'

We cut through the no man's land of boarded-up shops and scruffy B&Bs in the shadow of the Westway. The grey concrete of Trellick Tower reminded me of my parents' block of flats. We turned into a residential street lined with late-Victorian dwellings in different states of disrepair and neglect. Their frontages sprouted satellite dishes like giant mushrooms, and TV sets blared through open windows in a cacophony of languages. Summerscale rang at the door of an unremarkable terraced house. There were footsteps inside and we felt, for what seemed like minutes, an eye examining us through the keyhole. A chubby little Maghrebian man finally opened the door. He was wearing a tracksuit almost identical to Summerscale's, and over it a long bournous with a pointed hood drooping halfway down his stout back.

'Mr Sumicale,' he said, looking at me, 'I expected you an hour ago.'

'Nick. A friend,' said Summerscale. 'Mahmoud Allaoui, my accountant.'

We shook hands. The suggestion that Summerscale's accountant would look like this, and live in a house like this, was preposterous, but I let it pass.

'Hey, Mahdi, I know. I am sorry.' Summerscale patted the 'accountant' on the shoulder.

A woman appeared in the lobby behind the man. She raised her right hand and showed four fingers then two, before Allaoui had time to turn. A brunette in her late thirties, she was dressed in a tight silk dress printed with irises positioned so that the blue flowers opened around her ample breasts like huge hands supporting their milky volume, while the green stems were gathered in a bouquet around her plump waist. Her skin was like porcelain and she showed acres of it. I couldn't take my eyes off her chest.

Allaoui frowned and pushed her through one of the side doors. She gave a little yelp but stayed out of sight. He made no attempt to explain her presence. He took a padded envelope from a deep pocket in his cloak and handed it to Summerscale.

As we weaved our way back to Chelsea in a Land Rover, which he described as 'his little car', Summerscale started talking about Natalia again. Alongside the idea of the gallery he had suggested staging a one-off exhibition of Russian art in aid of Siberian orphanages, hoping that it would give her a taste for that kind of activity. He talked of it all as though I was already fully up to date. I wondered if she had misled him about me in some way, to create an impression that she was doing something concrete about her gallery or her exhibition.

'The art loan is not a problem. We spoke to the Americans and the Russians and even to the Swiss. It's the space we're after at the moment. Each installation requires a room of its own, more or less, and she doesn't want just any old warehouse. She goes on about the "poetics of space" as if we hadn't had enough of old Gery Feng-Shui-ing The Laurels to death. It may all come to nothing but I'd like Nat to keep herself busy. You know what they say: the devil finds work for idle hands.'

I did not expect to become Summerscale's drinking buddy after that outing, but he had different ideas. Some days later, he stopped at Fynch's to invite me to one of those pretentious new restaurants in Soho where the food costs a hundred pounds a head and the cheapest bottle of wine twice as much. I assumed that I was part of some renewed matchmaking plot involving Gery, but it was the prospect of Natalia's presence that made me put on my best suit.

The restaurant was heaving. It took a moment to see Summerscale at a table, flanked by two women.

'Nick, old boy, how good of you to join us,' he said as I took my seat. I am sure I was right in detecting a trace of mockery in his voice. The women – the brunette we saw at Allaoui's and someone looking very much like her but with more make-up – beamed at me. In their cheerful tight dresses, with their elaborate hairdos and carefully manicured nails, they looked like a couple of secretaries on an evening out with their patrician boss. I could begin to imagine why Summerscale was taking the wife of his so-called accountant out to an expensive dinner, but I was curious to find out what I and the other woman had to do with it.

Summerscale introduced them as Janice and Sal. 'Mrs Allaoui,' Janice added with a hint of mischief. She proffered her hand at a slight angle as though she was half-expecting me to kiss it. They explained that they were sisters and shrieked with joy when I was unable to guess which one was the elder. There was a five-year gap. Mrs Allaoui asked me to guess her age. I mentioned a number in the low thirties.

'Wrong! Wrong! You are almost a decade out, Nicky love,' she laughed.

There was a look at the back of her eyes that suggested she wasn't convinced by my flattery but that she was mistaken as to its aims. She was clearly used to being desired by men, used to lustful preambles.

They were two of the most cheerfully vulgar creatures I have ever had the luck to meet, but they knew a great deal about food and wine. They analysed and admired each plateful and shrieked with delight over each fancy culinary trick: sprinklings of golden caviar, oysters suspended in sea water *en gelée*, baskets woven out of rare herbs containing mouthfuls of cheese coated in slivers of white truffle.

They recognised touches they had seen on *Masterchef* and in the pages of glossy magazines, and they sniffed and slurped their wine like two cocker spaniels. Every now and then Janice would lift a forkful to Summerscale's mouth, pursing her lips like a mother moving her child on to solid food. He relished the attention and shot a quick wink in my direction each time he took a mouthful. I was too baffled by the spectacle to be outraged.

Whenever the sommelier uncorked a new bottle, it was Janice who tried it. She raised the glass high in the air to inspect the colour against the light, then buried her nose deep inside the rim and finally took a sip and mulled it in her purple-coloured mouth. And all the while, her right hand tinkled and jingled with bracelets, while her left, decorated with several large rings, rested high on Summerscale's thigh. Her sister leaned towards me, hitching up the pink straps of her bra and smiling coquettishly. I pretended not to notice.

Amid such merriment we finished a third bottle and opened a fourth. Although he had invited me, I felt I should at least offer to share the bill, yet even a half of it was probably getting close to my monthly wage. Summerscale and the women laughed more and more loudly, although you wouldn't have noticed it. The whole restaurant was generating a lecherous cacophony, which reverberated from its bare floors and walls.

Janice and Summerscale became more openly tactile. Under the table, she caressed his leg with her plump little foot. She latched onto each of his repartees as though it was the funniest thing anyone had ever said. If you took class out of the equation, this brash and almost hysterically cheerful Englishwoman looked more like Summerscale's wife while Natalia could be his young mistress.

I was beginning to feel quite morose. Sal was looking restless.

'Our Tommy bought Janice a little flat in Covent Garden, the cutest little flat. A place for all of us to have a little fun.' She pressed my hand close to her breast. Under the silk of her dress, I could feel the padded cup of her bra caving in under my knuckles.

'I am going to disappear for a moment,' Summerscale interrupted. 'Look after the ladies, Nick, will you?'

The moment he left, Sal and Janice engaged in a quick whispering exchange. Then Janice turned to me and said, 'So how do you know our Tom, then, Nicky darling?'

Before I had any time to answer, she said, 'Look at him, here he comes, quick as a flash, my sweet boy.'

Summerscale was brimming with newfound energy.

He had already paid the bill, in spite of my insisting on sharing it, and we were walking towards Covent Garden. The two sisters were hanging on Summerscale's arms and teetering on the high heels of their strappy sandals, while their pedicured toes shone white and plump in the glare of the streetlights, like rows of tiny new potatoes. Summerscale looked as if he was enjoying the walk.

It was Sal, by now the drunker of the two women, who leaned towards me. She was so close that her tongue touched my earlobe as she spoke. Her breath was a mixture of alcoholic mist and some sweet powdery scent that was not altogether unpleasant.

'How do you know our Tommy, then, Nick, my love?' Sal repeated her sister's question.

'I am a friend of—'

'What a jolly place that was,' Summerscale said, cutting me off. 'We must do it more often.'

'Oh, the ice-maiden,' Janice laughed. 'Are you from Siberia too, then, Nicky dear?'

She seemed to find the notion hilarious.

'Shut up, Janice.' Summerscale pushed her quite forcefully. She teetered, stunned out of her drunkenness for a moment, but not enough to make me think this was the first time. A dark shadow flitted over our little group. I felt the drink seep out of me.

'Tommy,' Janice said, her voice sweet and pleading. 'Mum doesn't mean it, Tommy.'

That Janice Allaoui was Summerscale's mistress, there was no doubt. They looked disappointed for a moment when I bid my farewell at the top of St Martin's Lane and refused a nightcap. Sal planted a sloppy kiss on my earlobe, whispering something about *another time*, but seemed contented enough to hang on Summerscale's left arm while Jan clasped the right.

'Leaving me to look after both girls, you schmuck,' he

said; then, switching to Russian: 'I guessed that much, you limp Serbian dick. It's my wife you dream of shafting, no?'

He did not look angry at all. He looked like someone who would cope without me. The women laughed although they had no idea what he was saying. As they went, tottering, on their way to his bachelor pad, Sal turned towards me and threw me one last drunken wink.

The night air was bracing. It was well after midnight, yet London was anything but asleep. Buses were full of people, windows were lit, many of the shops were still open. The town smelled of grilled meat, pickles, beer, vomit and piss. The whole bloody place was the image of Janice and Sal, I thought as I sobered up: disgusting in theory, and yet somehow at ease with its own lust. Somehow not unpleasant at all.

In one of the Mayfair art galleries, a party was in full swing. A tall thin girl held a martini glass with a plump olive floating in it. She beckoned me inside. Her eyes shone darkly on a wide, heart-shaped face. I hesitated for a moment but went on my way.

Arab boys drove slowly up and down Knightsbridge in their expensive cars, on the prowl for good times. On Brompton Road Harrods looked like the mirage of a cruise liner outlined in fairy lights. In South Kensington, the streets slowly grew quieter, and the air started to smell of garden compost and flowers.

The silhouette of Gorsky's palace, still incomplete and uninhabited but already almost as imposing as St Paul's Cathedral, came into view. I had nearly gone past when I noticed Gorsky's distinctive limousine waiting. One of his bodyguards stepped out and held open the kerb-side door. Gorsky emerged from the building site, flanked by two other guards. Without noticing me he stepped into the car. He raised the hem of his expensive coat. As his long lean thighs swung into the seat, just below the rim of his jacket I noticed the white fringes of a prayer shawl.

4

The thick envelope lined with silver tissue contained an elaborately embossed invitation. My name was written using archaic phonetic spelling: Nicholas Kimowitch Esq. I knew about the Serpentine summer parties only from photographs in colour supplements. Some of Fynch's customers, those whose names graced the list of donors on the walls of big museums, occasionally talked about them. I recognised these men and women in photographs captioned with quadruple-barrelled names, wearing family jewels and holding champagne flutes, or standing uncomfortably next to celebrities *du jour*, models, starlets, duchesses, and assorted mistresses of oligarchs, rock stars and Hollywood moguls.

I was familiar with some of the pavilions designed to grace the lawn by the Serpentine Gallery through the summer months. These transitory architectural follies were opened with grand events of which this was one, but I had usually experienced them later, among the tourists, sipping a glass of lemonade under a shaded roof or staring at them slantwise from the nearby deckchairs which normally accommodate dozens of burkaed women spending their summers and sometimes Ramadan away from the blaze and public austerities of the Gulf.

Folly was indeed an apt name for the edifice that rose from the grassy field that year. It was by far the largest and probably the most expensive pavilion ever, and it was designed by the same Chinese woman who had recently completed a new dining area for the Metropolitan Museum in New York, and whose name was on the hoardings that shielded Gorsky's building site. Her pavilion looked like a cross between a Russian monastery and a flying saucer. Exquisite layers of red, brown and ochre tiles covered its walls. Its onion domes shone above the treetops like a Byzantine Camelot, soaring towards the night sky in luscious aquamarine, emblazoned with huge golden stars.

Russian money was rumoured to be behind it all: the pavilion, the party and the invitations. Although it was difficult to guess anything from the name of the upmarket PR agency which handled the RSVPs, I assumed that the money must be Gorsky's, the pavilion an outrider for his own Camelot a verst or two to the south.

You could hear the sounds of laughter and jazz rising into the night sky even before you crossed Kensington Gore, and you could smell a mixture of expensive musky scents and rare flowers long before you handed over your invitation and progressed through the X-rays and layers of security. The British needed protecting from any number of species of terrorist who hated them only marginally less – or more, depending on the cause – than the Americans and the Israelis; the Russians needed protecting from themselves; and the celebrities from lunatics who brooded darkly on the internet devising one-off celebrity bids of their own. Expensive cars with liveried drivers lined the perimeter, and the bodyguards not allowed inside rested in them, on call, talking to each other, or playing with their hi-tech tablets. Once you were in, you instantly realised that you were *in*, perhaps for the first time in your entire wretched life.

Dozens of waiting staff flitted among the guests, beautiful boys and girls dressed in identical black and white costumes designed by the architect herself to look vaguely Asiatic and tailored more expensively than those worn by guests at an upscale English wedding party. Some carried magnums of white and pink champagne; others held trays with colourful cocktails and fresh juices; or crystal glasses filled with iced tea, with exotic flowers slowly opening at the bottom. Yet others appeared with flat lacquered boards bearing tiny thimbles of spirits and liqueurs I did not even begin to recognise.

'Château d'Yquem,' shouted Christopher Fynch against the noise, while glancing down at the glasses of dessert wine he was holding in each hand. 'Someone told me there were several dozen cases of 1947 and 1959, the great vintages.'

A young woman wearing a dress made of silver thread

as fine as spider silk tripped and fell into a boat-load of black and albino caviar which was rocking gently in a cradle carved out of a single enormous block of ice. She sat up and carefully removed beads of roe from her cleavage. Two men rushed to help her get up, but when they saw that she was happy to stay there, they started licking the tiny eggs off her outstretched palms. Camera flashes sparkled in the mist of the outdoor refrigeration that enveloped the scene. An orchestra played Shostakovich's Waltz No. 2 somewhere in the background.

High above us, London stars twinkled faintly and planes continued to fly west towards Heathrow in a steady, stately procession. Everything around me, even that girl's fall, was harmoniously orchestrated, beautiful to look at, yet the cumulative effect was melancholy, as though some unquenchable thirst lurked at the heart of it all.

Had I known who *le tout Londres* was, I would no doubt have been able to confirm that it was there. I recognised a number of men and women, all looking slightly and unsettlingly different from their more familiar avatars of the printed page and television screen:

the new priesthood of tight-lipped directors of big art galleries looking like illustrations from *Foxe's Book of Martyrs* – notwithstanding their expensive dinner jackets and bow ties; famous journalists and writers flushed from too much champagne; captains of industry; politicians; actors; models; and all of them talking, laughing, shaking hands, exchanging contact details, pursing their lips for air kisses, looking for more tempting prey and moving on, always moving on.

I was standing on my own watching a *son et lumière* show, which depicted the story of Russian art from Kievan Rus to the present, when a pair of hands covered my eyes. In her severe black dress with a little white collar, Gery Pekarova looked like a schoolgirl and laughed like a boy whose voice had just broken. She embraced me as though we were the oldest of friends. Her dress was covered in sequins, which crackled faintly against my body like rice-paper confetti.

'I haven't seen Mrs Summerscale in such a long while. Is she here?'

She looked puzzled.

'You must be joking. Natalia coming to a Russian

party! Her Russia is all abstract – art and music, mist and mirrors – but when it comes to the Russians it's always *Nyet spasibo* – no thank you. They remind her of all the things she wants to forget, she says. I am not sure if she even opened her invitation. I had to cadge mine as someone's companion. Some Russian guy I shook off the moment we passed security.'

'You know it's a Gorsky party, don't you?' she continued. 'I wouldn't have missed it if I had to kill to get in – and probably some of the guests have done just that! The whole of London talks about his parties. Last year he hired one of those huge clubs in Pall Mall and had the façade covered in trailing orchids. Then there was that ice rink they created in Kensington Gardens, buried in a nest of pine and holly: like a huge Christmas wreath, dark green, with shiny red baubles. It was January thirteenth, the Russian New Year's Eve. They encouraged people to take the baubles away at the end of the evening. A tipsy Bulgarian friend of mine flung several into the Serpentine; stone skipping, she said, silly fool. A few days later someone told her that each was worth a couple of thousand pounds.

'Another time he flew people on private jets to Italy and took them sailing on his yacht, all the way from Genoa to Sardinia. I mislead you when I say he took them: people kept guessing when he was going to turn up, but he stayed in the Highlands, playing golf in the rain. You don't see him anywhere. They say he watches his own parties via webcam. Well, so long as it floats his boat . . .'

She looked up towards an imaginary security camera and cupped her little breasts. Her English was accented yet determinedly colloquial, and her gestures were charmingly incongruous too. She nodded to mean no and shook her head to mean yes, in the unique way that Bulgarians do, but her hands, with their bony fingers and long crimson nails, moved like the hands of a rapper.

'You get used to money in this town,' she added, 'but Gorsky's money is beyond all dreams of wealth. No one knows exactly how he made it. Some say oil, some say weapons. Russian or Chinese. I've heard people suggest that he is a Russian spy and that he is a fugitive, hunted by Russian agents. Friends tell me that he was once arrested in Bulgaria while trying to deliver weapons to Serbia – or possibly export weapons from Serbia, I can't remember – and that he bribed his way out of jail. I heard that he studied in St Petersburg with the Bulgarian president and that they are the best of mates. Or was it the Romanian one? Who knows, Nick? Who cares?'

She produced her business card from a tiny clutch bag and tucked it into my trouser pocket. Her fingers remained there until she felt my penis move, and then she beamed at me and walked away. I made no effort to follow. Her dress caught the light and shimmered like a bituminous pool on her suntanned skin.

As I walked back towards Kensington Gore, the silver limousine drew up in front of me. A man sitting next to the driver jumped out and held the back door open.

'Mr Kimović?' he said. 'If you please.'

I saw the familiar figure of Roman Gorsky inside. He patted the seat next to him.

'I hope you enjoyed the party.' He nodded towards the screen in front, which was broadcasting scenes from the place I had just left.

'I have never seen its like.'

'Did you meet any friends?'

'No, unless you count my boss and Gery Pekarova,' I said.

'Ah, the gymnast,' Gorsky interrupted. 'I may have had the honour. I am old enough to remember her as a young girl, gold medal around her neck. She was so pretty. The steroids have wreaked havoc, but she is still most striking, I believe. Isn't London strange, the way it brings us back together? You are from Belgrade, you said? I was often in Belgrade in the nineties. Difficult times. Everything rationed. No electricity. Military helicopters flying low above the town ferrying wounded from the battlefields. The hospitals lacked everything, even the most basic supplies.'

'I left long before the worst. Who could have guessed it?' I was cautious. I hardly wanted to cross him inadvertently.

'Anyone could,' he countered. 'The second the Wall went down in Berlin, it was clear. Your nation is a victim of the Cold War, Mr Kimović. Much misunderstood. Like mine. At least mine can stand up for itself.'

We drove slowly past tall Victorian façades that shimmered like sea cliffs in the moonlight. Behind them, people dined, watched television, made love or slept. They knew about men like Gorsky only from the gossip columns. He surveyed the streetscapes as he spoke and occasionally asked the driver to slow down so that he could take in a portico or a row of high windows.

'I love architecture,' he said. 'Remember that when you are buying books for me. Robert Adam's studies of Diocletian's palace perhaps? I saw a sketch in my university library; long before I thought I'd ever see the Adriatic. Nothing too technical, though. I am a mathematician by training. Mathematics is closer to poetry than to the other sciences, perhaps. Or to philosophy. Pure abstraction. Like money, you might say.'

He did not expect a reply.

'I used to teach in Leningrad, before all this. I wrote a doctoral thesis about the discovery of transfinite numbers. Some of those mathematicians got a bit carried away by abstraction. They became Name Worshippers: they believed that the name of God is God himself – the very "word" that opens the Bible. Rationalism taken as far as it would go, so far that it turns into its own opposite, into mysticism. I had problems because of that work. It was seen as the study of religion, not mathematics. I nearly lost my job and, in Russia, you know, you never just lose your job, you have to make all sorts of compromises.'

He waved his right hand as though he was chasing the thought away.

'Don't you just love London? Centuries of uninterrupted cash-flow. All that historic, uncountable money, chests and chests of it, from the four corners of the world . . .'

His head turned towards the Natural History Museum.

'But I don't like the English,' he continued. 'They have an amphibian quality, a slipperiness that comes of their squatting on an island, able to evade the grasp of their neighbours.' I expected him to elaborate. I was fond of the English on the whole and it did not seem that he had anything much to do with them, but I was not going to argue. He fell silent.

The interior of the car smelled of wood and leather and, wafting from the front seats, an expensive eau de cologne. The driver or the bodyguard, I couldn't tell: both their suits and their hair were more impressively cut than mine. The two men stared wordlessly ahead as we changed lanes or overtook other vehicles. They exchanged a quick whisper in Russian only when a cyclist rested his hand on our car at the traffic light. The insouciance seemed staggering. The bodyguard glanced into the side-view mirror on his left. His right arm moved. I saw his shoulders flex then relax. I looked back as we pulled away. It was a boy of fourteen or fifteen, his pale face under the cycle helmet so freckled that it looked like a speckled egg under the streetlamps.

Gorsky was too absorbed by the bluish screen in front of us to notice anything. It was transmitting the end of the party. He nodded at the driver and the car filled with the music of Bach. The sound quality was ethereal. Although it was far from loud, we heard no other noise. As we glided along the streets people tried to look inside. Some paused at the kerb and took photographs of the vehicle.

Gorsky searched in the glove compartment built into the wide armrest between us and produced a small box which he handed over, snapping it open. A medal rested on a dark satin cushion.

'Have a look. See what it says at the back.'

I lifted a familiar white cross.

'*To R. B. Gorsky, from the grateful Serbian nation*', read the engraving in fine Cyrillic calligraphy.

He took the medal from my hand, examined it for a moment as though he was about to share its story, but instead laid it carefully back into its box, which he closed again with another soft snap.

At some point in my life, I ceased to care about its course sufficiently to take any decisive action. Something in me became unmoored; I disengaged. I made no virtue of escaping the Yugoslav wars by a whisker. Had my mother not refused my call-up papers, had I been mobilised, I would have gone to shoot and be shot at.

I realise that this is a strange way of explaining how – or why – I started seeing Gery Pekarova. The correct – blunt – thing to say would be that she started fucking me. I wasn't actively attracted, but I didn't mind her company, which is more than I can say about most people. I think she felt the same for me. She must have sensed that I was the sort of man who did not mind being summoned, did not mind doing as he was told, particularly if it involved no hard work. I became her phone-in, takeaway friend.

She was an amoral creature, and that was clear to me from the start. I am not sure how she came to live in a large-ish council flat with a view of St Luke's in Chelsea, the sort of property that would cost a seven-figure sum if it were sold on the open market, but you could safely bet it involved telling more than one lie. I sometimes saw her jogging along in the side streets, dressed in a zipped Lycra body suit, like a deep sea diver. Like everything about her, her hard feline shape was simultaneously attractive and repellent.

We bumped into each other in Waitrose on the King's Road. Her shopping basket contained a box of sprouting broccoli and a bottle of vodka, mine an Indian meal for one.

'Nikita,' she gurgled. I realised that her Mick Jagger face must have resembled Nastassja Kinski's when she – and Nastassja – were younger.

'We must get together again, Nikita, go out, dance, have fun.'

So we got together. We went to a cheap Bulgarian grill off Green Lanes, then to an expensive Bulgarian club in a basement off Piccadilly Circus.

The first was full of men who looked like pub bouncers and who munched mouthfuls of meat mournfully while staring at a huge TV screen which belted out the music of homesickness from the corner. Gery pushed a piece of grilled chicken around her plate while urging me to consume the mountain of pork and lamb she had ordered for me.

The club, when we reached it soon after midnight, was heaving with beautiful people, sharply dressed and self-consciously elegant – a different Bulgaria altogether – handsome dark-haired men and women who looked as though they were auditioning for the role of James Bond and his latest squeeze. Most of them seemed to know Gery. She was an amazing dancer. I wish I could say the same about myself. Before we entered that place, I thought us a reasonable match; the balance, if anything, was on my side. Here, I suddenly wondered what she was doing with me.

At four a.m., she took me home. She took me. I am not a vastly promiscuous man, but I have had enough lovers to appreciate Gery's love-making skills; indeed, with her assistance, I demonstrated my appreciation four times between four and eight, when I finally fell asleep, somehow hitting the mattress with a thud and feeling as though I was continuing to fall at the same time.

I once read a biography of Mrs Simpson, ordered by one of Fynch's most faithful customers. The author hinted slyly at a bag of tricks the future Duchess of Windsor had picked up from the brothel culture of Shanghai. I imagine that they had something akin to Gery Pekarova's knowledge of male anatomy in mind, but the Duchess could not have rivalled Gery's feats of internal gymnastics. Gery could do things that I did not think physically possible. Our 'love-making' was heavy on tricks and light on connection: we remained two separate people masturbating together.

'We are friends with benefits, aren't we, Nicky?' she said,

with that self-congratulatory smile she adopted whenever she appropriated an English cliché. Now she kept the English word for benefits but used the Bulgarian for friends. It was practically the same as in my mother tongue. The sound alone triggered a wave of warmth starting somewhere around my solar plexus. I took her head in my hands. This felt more intimate than anything we had been doing moments before. She pushed me away, laughing.

'Don't go soft on me now, Nikolai,' she said. 'It's too late.' Then she closed her eyes and fell asleep.

We awoke at midday and rested on her enormous bed listening to church bells. She laughed when I told her I thought she was a lesbian when we first met.

'Perhaps I am, too . . . Perhaps I like you because you are such a girl's blouse, Nikita.'

She stretched her long body and then lifted her right leg into the air, whistling a Serbian – or perhaps Bulgarian – tune. Each muscle took shape individually under her taut skin. Her toenails were covered in black varnish. A thin white line cut across her hips, the stencil of a thong. She held my chin, kissed me and went to take a shower.

Outside, a drizzly afternoon hung half-heartedly above Chelsea like a semi-deflated balloon. I stared at the ceiling, composing, as I so often did these days, my shopping list for Roman Gorsky. I had just acquired pristine first editions of *À la Recherche* and *Ulysses*, and a rare Soviet samizdat typescript of *Dr Zhivago* in a walnut sewing box carved especially to hide the sheaves of fading carbon copy. Under an ornate lid, the top chamber still contained needles, threads and thimbles, and a half-finished sampler of embroidery.

Such finds notwithstanding, the Russians remained a problem. The whole Modernist canon was published on cheap paper. Mid-century books were yellow and brittle and fell apart, newer stuff came in inferior bindings – neither had the look my patron was after. Given the amounts of money I had at my disposal, I could order books to be set, in a print-run of one, especially for him, in Belgrade. My university friends were now working as printers for two hundred euros a month. Gorsky was spending more each second.

'A kopek for your thoughts.' Gery stood in the doorway wrapped in a white towelling robe.

'Gorsky,' I said. 'I wonder why he wants the library.'

She curled next to me and sighed.

'Do you think I stand a chance? I know they like sixteen-year-olds, people like him – fresh cunt – but they must get bored with those fuckwits. I've been to one or two parties where they had teenage girls lined up along the wall, like those seafood displays in French brasseries, yet those men just kept talking about their business, paying no attention. Gorsky looks like a cold fish to me, but he is not married apparently. A woman can get used to loneliness inside a marriage given other compensations. What do you think, Niki? I know his world well. What does a sixteen-year-old know?'

I couldn't imagine any other woman weighing her chances with the richest man in London so openly and so soon after she had made love to me, but, with Gery, this made absolute sense. I was, almost, charmed by her lack of pretence.

I wasn't sure if I was doing him or her a favour when I invited her to join me at the opera. The tickets were a present from Gorsky. I had just managed to secure a first edition of Pushkin's *Eugene Onegin* dedicated to Prince Dolgoruky. Gorsky wanted it, but so did a number of other oligarchs who entered the bidding. Fynch's commission for that purchase alone was not unadjacent to our usual annual turnover. Gorsky was so delighted to have the volume that I was granted a rare glimpse into his personal life.

'A woman who means a great deal to me knew . . . knows still, perhaps . . . the whole of *Onegin* by heart.'

He hesitated for a moment, on the brink of saying more, but changed his mind and proceeded to tell me how he had donated ten million pounds to the Royal Opera on condition that they close the season with *Eugene Onegin*. We gathered a couple of hours before the performance in one of those grand hotel restaurants in Mayfair which seem forever empty when you look in from the street. Gorsky had a private salon. He was already seated when I arrived, turning a thimble of vodka around its axis in his long, elegant hand. The digits on his watch kept catching the light. His head was so majestic when he was seated in that way that he looked even taller than he was. The mirrors reflected his blond crown and his black jacket in a sort of *mise en abyme*, as though he was at the heart of a kaleidoscope.

The waiter was still fussing with my coat when Gery made her entrance. She was wearing a tight silver dress – another sequined number – which made her look like a mermaid. She wore heels so towering that although she was five inches shorter, they made her seem taller than me. Her teeth looked even more brilliantly white than usual because her skin had bronzed considerably since I saw her the day before. Her long black hair was held in a silver net, through which individual curls fell as if by accident. She looked more like a transvestite than ever: the effect was somewhere between stunning and ridiculous.

'Roman Borisovich Gorsky. Gergana Pekarova,' I introduced them to each other. Gorsky stood up and kissed her outstretched hand. If they had met before, neither signalled it.

I don't know how many languages he spoke. Each seemed almost perfect but none sounded like his mother tongue. He peppered both his English and his Russian with French and Italian. In his car, after the Serpentine party, I heard him answer a telephone call in fluent German. He now spoke Bulgarian, with a soft Russian accent, but fluently nonetheless.

'Oh, I lived in Sofia for three or four years,' he explained when she expressed surprise on hearing him address her in her mother tongue. 'You would have been in Germany by then.'

Gery did not seem taken aback by his knowledge of the details of her defection. She was barely out of her teens and still a world champion when she slipped her minders in Munich, she had told me. He did not explain what he was doing in Sofia.

He continued to turn his glass of vodka without drinking any. Gery ordered some champagne but did not drink it either. I alone was slowly getting tipsy on both vodka and champagne. After the waiters started bringing platefuls of sashimi, I was the only one eating too. I drifted in and out of their Bulgarian conversation.

'And what do you do in London?' Gery asked.

'I am doing up a house by the Thames,' Gorsky said. 'And you?'

'I work as a personal trainer and a nutritionist.'

'Oh,' said Gorsky, 'I need both . . .'

'I take only one client at a time. That means I can be available to travel. People of excellence don't like to drop their routine wherever they are. It would take a lot to tempt me to leave my client at the moment.'

'I can offer a lot,' Gorsky said. They both seemed deadly serious. It was difficult to know what exactly they were negotiating.

'My client is a very distinguished lady. A lady of excellence. I am devoted to her. You put me in a difficult situation, Mr Gorsky. I am more comfortable with women. Professionally, I mean.'

Her manicured hand now hovered above his lapel. Under the table, her foot was climbing up my shin and along my femur at an angle that only an Olympic gold medallist could accomplish.

It was raining heavily when we walked out of the restaurant and took the car to Covent Garden. Along Piccadilly, tourists sheltered from the weather in shopping arcades.

Gery sat between us looking – in her silver spangled outfit – as though she was part of the luxurious interior. Her left hand rested on my knee, her right on Gorsky's. There was an unusual ring on her right hand, diamond-encrusted, in the shape of a snake. Her hair smelled of jasmine oil. For some reason, they chatted about chocolate and marzipan; how neither of them had tasted the good stuff until they were in their twenties. When she turned towards me her eyes shone in the semi-darkness with a mixture of life force and undisguised greed.

The opera was tucked away modestly in a side street, dispensing with the panache of the grand European houses which sit proudly in the middle of their own huge squares and glimmer under their golden domes. Few things unrelated to battlefields seemed to merit proper squares in London; even parliament faced only a medium-sized traffic junction. Inside, too, the opera was pokier and less glitzy than I expected, and there were enough tourists with little rucksacks on their backs to make even my cheap jacket seem elegant. I had no intention of trying to upgrade my wardrobe to suit my new friends, and my clothes troubled neither of them in the least.

As Gorsky took his place in the corner of his box and started flicking through the programme, I became aware how famous – infamous perhaps – he actually was. The lorgnettes from the stalls turned towards our box, as though in some costume drama. People stared while pretending not to look. He may have been the most discreet of London oligarchs – no Premier League football clubs to his name, no high-profile divorces, no attempted assassinations either of him or, as far as anyone knew, commissioned by him – but despite, or because of, his persistent absence, his parties, and the palace for which I was equipping the library, assured him regular appearances in the gossip columns. His face was as familiar as those of Abramovich and Berezovsky. The lack of a personal story became a story in its own right. Was he gay, perhaps? In a country like Russia no amount of money bought freedom from homophobia, journalists insinuated slyly, while disingenuously protecting their own liberal credentials. Why was he so determinedly alone?

The noise of tuning instruments from the orchestra pit slowly rose above the murmurs of the audience. There was a roar of applause and the young conductor stood in front of the musicians. In deepest silence, members of the chorus dressed as Russian peasants gradually filled the stage and then the song of the field labourers rose towards the gods. The staging was amazing, like nothing I had imagined, although I knew the story well. There were two Tatianas. The older one sang about love and sorrow; the younger one danced, mute. She had yet to fall in love, yet to know the pain of it. I cast a furtive glance towards my companions. Gery's eyes were fixed on the stage, her body leaned forward, her eyes moving from one performer to the other, but I could already sense her restlessness. This was not her scene. Gorsky was reclining, half hidden by the shadow of the red velvet that draped our box. His eyes were slowly welling with tears.

Slav soul, I thought, with a dash of unjustified mockery, for while I was one myself, he was not, even though he was marinated in Slav culture. I had assumed that he was staring into the darkness above people's heads, but then an instinct made me follow the line of his gaze across the auditorium towards the row of boxes opposite. Directly in his sights there was a group of young men and women, city types, looking at each other over their champagne glasses far more than they looked at the stage. One couple was sharing a kiss. In the smaller box to the left, there were just two people, a man and a woman. The man's face was hidden by the programme. The faint blue light emanating from behind it suggested that he was examining his mobile phone. The woman was wearing a simple black dress, with no jewellery to offset its severity or shine against her translucent skin. She clutched a small purse against her chest. There was no doubt about it: unlike most of the rest of us, she was there for the music. Her familiar, beautiful Russian face was unmistakeable.

5

I heard about it from Victor, Fynch said. He told me it was almost Spartan by Gorsky's standards, but the man was so discreet about his invitations that you wouldn't be startled to find Putin lunching with Julia Roberts under the pines. The guest list had never been leaked to anyone: none of those vulgar little name-drops in gossip columns, ever. Not once. You wouldn't know the island was there unless you looked at the map.

Victor acted as a sort of caretaker for the oligarchs when they first arrived in London. I suppose you could put a first in Russian from Cambridge to better use, but rarely to a more profitable one. They came to Britain with suitcases loaded with cash; he helped them get a house, furnish it, put their children into the best schools, sort out everything from their visas to their parking fines. Ten per cent commission. They did not even notice it. A UK visa: how many would you need, sir? Your best friend's daughter is coming to stay with you . . . alone? She is sixteen, you said? Will that be six months or a year? We'll try our very best, sir. A new nose or a new pair of breasts for the lady wife who doesn't speak a word of English? Certainly, sir. We'll get a five-star hospital with a resident interpreter.

Victor made a pretty penny but it all went to his first wife and her little place in Petersham, or so he said. And she didn't even allow him to see the kids. He slept in Fynch's bookshop for the best part of a month when she locked him out of the house. He was too depressed even to book a hotel at first, he claimed: dossing chimed with the state of his soul. Then Gorsky took a shine to him and ordered him to stay in his flat at the Barbican. This was when Victor was sorting out financial arrangements for the Barracks and dining out with the estate agent.

Not that there was any danger of being gazumped, since Bill Gates and the Emir of Qatar were about the only other people in the world who could afford the place. At the Barbican, Victor flourished, took some girls out and then in, got over the divorce, updated his dance moves, pretended the flat was his. He wouldn't hear a word against Gorsky. And, come to think of it, he had probably played his part in our book-buying commission: he and Fynch go back to the same house in that Thames-side school they never allowed me to mention in public. I sometimes wondered if Fynch might have known something about the library even before that day when Gorsky walked into the shop, but had neglected to mention it. He treated everything that Victor accomplished or promised as a joke. That he also refused to 'talk shop' with me would have been amusing, had the shop not been our shared business.

I did not get to ask Fynch how formal he thought the island was. It was irrelevant, anyway. I wasn't about to go shopping for clothes. I was flattered that Gorsky had invited me – to talk books and plans, he said vaguely

– but I was sure that he knew I wasn't about to up the sartorial ante. I was broke.

The day he issued the invitation was as drizzly as it gets in London and I had just spent a great deal of his money on some Russian incunabula which mysteriously appeared for sale in an auction, offered by an anonymous seller in Buenos Aires. Why not take a few days off, old boy? Why not relax? Gorsky suggested when he rang to congratulate me, though my achievement was simply in finding out the date of the sale.

Over in Greece, for example, the temperature was already in the high twenties, he said.

I hate travelling and I hate hotels, I responded, even the best ones, all that palaver, booking, transfers, hours and hours. I had barely left London in the last fifteen years. At first I couldn't travel because of my papers, then the very idea of travel started to feel tiring. Gorsky just laughed.

This was simple. A car to Battersea, then the helicopter, then the private plane. And a fresh bottle of champagne at each stage if I wanted it: by the time we reached the airport I no longer knew which airport I was in, though I could see it wasn't Heathrow. Judging from the architecture it could have been Stansted, but it was empty. My meagre luggage was whisked away. I was left with a panama hat which I had bought at some expense at Bates in Jermyn Street and which I now held in a dark blue tube like an Olympic torch.

I had my own UKBA checker at what passed for a passport desk. And a newsagent all to myself. I didn't even have to pay, just sign off for the papers with my flight code. I was a solo traveller, it seems. At one point I noticed a woman coming through a huge sliding door. Someone carried several hat boxes a couple of steps behind her. She was tall and she looked even taller because of her vast turquoise turban. I couldn't guess her ethnicity. Her face was so taut her skin could have been stapled at the back. That was the only non-uniformed person I had come across since Gorsky's driver buzzed on my front door to collect me. She did not even notice me: why would she?

The jet was something, too. Two hostesses waited on

standby to strap me into my armchair for take-off. I could have chosen a chaise longue, but the recliner seemed good enough for a four-hour flight. I fell asleep while the pilot was still reciting the names of some Belgian and German towns we were going to fly over, and I woke up above the bluest sea, the European mainland nowhere in view, just an archipelago of small islands with white houses scattered on them like sugar cubes. There was still time for the blonde stewardess with her coquettishly tilted red toque to recite a choice of light refreshments. I asked for a bowl of pineapple sorbet and she delivered it with a silver spoon and a crystal glass of icy vodka on the side. The linen napkin had the initials RBG embroidered in silver thread: the same familiar monogram I spied on the cuff of her white shirt. It would have reminded one of slave ownership, but for the fact that they all appeared so thrilled to serve.

The Greek airport seemed even more deserted than the one I had left in Britain four hours previously. The true luxury of wealth is to be solitary in places where you least expect it. There was no luggage carousel.

There was no passport check and no customs. I walked through an empty, heavily air-conditioned building holding the tube containing my panama hat, feeling faintly ridiculous, towards another exit and another helicopter which flew me to Hesperos. There I was met by a golf buggy driven by a handsome Australian man in cricket whites. He delivered me into the hands of a stunning-looking Asian woman who walked me to my lodgings. I had long since lost count of the numbers of people Gorsky kept in full-time employment: three or four hundred perhaps, without even counting those in Russia who might actually be producing whatever he was trading in.

I was left in a low stone bungalow, a squat building hidden among flowering bushes, their crimson flowers so huge that they looked, on their perfect green lawn and against the perfect blue sea, like the set for a Greek episode of *Teletubbies*. I showered with what felt like sparkling water and splashed myself with a few drops of aftershave which I found in a glossy silk bag waiting on my bed. *Welcome to Hesperos, Mr Kimovic'*, read a card attached to it. Inside was a collection of goods one might need on a Greek island if one was a high-class rent boy who liked to travel extremely light: toiletries, suntan lotion, two pairs of swimming trunks, one minute and black, one baggy and printed in fetching blue and white stripes, flip-flops, a pair of white espadrilles, a slim camera and a pair of wraparound sunglasses. Everything came in my size, and from the kind of luxury brands I considered an utter waste of money. There was even an almost exact copy of my own panama hat.

Another card listed activities available on the island and daily excursions from it, and urged me not to hesitate to ask for snorkelling and scuba-diving equipment, wetsuits, sea-boarding and kite-surfing gear . . . a space ship, well . . . whatever took my fancy.

My bedside telephone rang. A female, sounding Scandinavian and apologetic, announced that dinner would be served in the main house, unless I preferred to dine alone. Out of curiosity, I resisted a temptation to stay on my own veranda with a tin of caviar from the fridge. I wanted to see who was sharing my Arcadia. But for the noisy lunacy of the crickets I could have been alone on the island.

When I found my way to the main villa, I was taken by its simplicity. Victor was not far wrong. By Roman Gorsky's standards, this was indeed an ascetic dwelling. It had once been an Ottoman pasha's palace, an Irish butler explained as he mixed my drink. In its simple symmetries, it could have been a stone house from a child's drawing: six windows on the first floor, four on the ground floor, two on each side of the wide green double doors in the centre, which were opened wide to reveal a wall-hanging with a hunting scene, flanked by tall candelabra on which shone a multitude of thick beeswax candles. Their scent blended with the wild thyme and tobacco smoke outside.

A wide pergola ran along the length of the veranda. From it trailed an old vine, its grapes still tiny and green. Half a dozen men had already gathered in its shade. Three sat in wicker armchairs half facing each other, three at an enormous stone table playing cards. I vaguely recognised a couple of British faces from the newspapers – the scion of a famous Jewish family who ran a lobbying firm but was more famous for his supermodel wife, and a former central banker who regularly cropped up on *Newsnight*. The lobbyist was suntanned, as though he had been on Hesperos for a while; the banker was as red as a freshly boiled lobster – the pages of the *Financial Times* he was leafing through paled beside his skin colour. There was a third man whom I took to be Spanish from his face and his raven-black hair, slickly oiled and combed close to his cranium, only to spill down over a gleaming white collar in a profusion of unruly locks.

The card players were indisputably Russian. They sat in shorts and tracksuit bottoms and an assortment of football shirts belonging to famous European clubs. They might have been at a holiday camp in their homeland, their synthetic sportswear comfortably accommodating their stocky forms, but here I wondered if they actually owned the teams. Clouds of cigarette smoke hung above the table. They looked up and nodded as I approached, barely interrupting their game. The Spaniard alone stood up. His heels clicked as he shook my hand. His stomach was as flat as a matador's. The banker and the lobbyist introduced themselves, then asked a few polite questions about the weather in London, without feigning any interest in my responses. The lobbyist's name was legendary – like Rothschild or Hilton. You did not assume there were people around who bore it, people you could actually meet. The banker's name was English and as monosyllabic as the man himself. His entire demeanour seemed intended to show that his visit to Hesperos was to be brief and that its purpose involved nothing other than business.

The Russians cursed vilely. One of them produced a thick wad of five-hundred-euro notes from a deep pocket in his tracksuit bottoms, and slammed it on the table, sending his cards into the bushes. Within seconds, an Indian man in a Mao jacket materialised and started to collect them. We were clearly being watched all the time, our desires guessed before we knew we had them.

I nursed my drink and looked down through the pines at the little port. A motorboat appeared as if from nowhere, with three women on board. They disembarked and climbed up the stone path towards the house. I could pick out their Russian conversation, the clicking of their heels on the stone and the rustle of the large, shiny shopping bags they carried. They did not even nod in my direction as they arrived. Each kissed a Russian man and each had her bottom groped or slapped proprietorially, and none seemed to mind. I wish I could say they were vulgar, but they were young and as interchangeable in their beauty and their elegance as their partners were in their cheerful crassness.

Gorsky was nowhere to be seen. Not that first evening, not the second, nor even the third. I lounged in a hammock, took a couple of scuba-diving classes and read thrillers from a small library in my bungalow. The lobbyist and the banker were getting more and more restless. The latter was on his phone all the time. The Russians occasionally dipped into the sea where they barked amicably at each other like a small group of walruses, then slumped in deckchairs, smoking and staring at the horizon. Their wives disappeared in their motorboat every morning and came back with more shopping from God knows where.

Finally, on my last evening, there was a barbeque party. Small boats brought guests from yachts moored across the archipelago. There were dozens of stunning young men and women who drank champagne, took cocaine, quite publicly, from silver boxes full of powder, and swam in the red glow of the dying sun. There was music from somewhere behind the trees – live, discreet music.

One of the young women gestured at me. I followed her along a path under the pines until we came to a low stone bench sheltered by wild jasmine. She lifted the hem of her white shirt-dress and pointed at her naked cunt. I had just enough time to register the low slit, rising barely a centimetre up her crotch, when she turned around and wiggled her bottom, then turned back again, pointing at her lips, pausing each time to raise an enquiring eyebrow. When she pressed her index finger on her cunt the second time, I nodded in consent, like an idiot at a fish stall. My trousers were beginning to hurt me.

She showed no sign of being either pleased or

disappointed by my choice. I guessed she spoke no English, and I wondered if she was mute as well. She hadn't said anything to anyone the whole evening. I assumed that she wasn't deaf because she danced rather nicely in her loose garment, raising her slim arms into the air to the sound of dozens of thin bracelets she wore on each wrist and ankle. They now jingled as she straddled me and moved her bottom backwards and forwards as I stared into the bouncy see-saw of her small breasts. Behind her, the dying sun was bathing everything in a deep, Saharan glow. It was extremely exciting in a surreal kind of way, beautiful and apocalyptic at the same time, because of the sheer decadence of our coupling. She was as moist as an oyster. I came very quickly. She sighed a little disappointed sigh, pulling a tissue out of the breast pocket of her dress and unfolding it to wipe between her legs, then suddenly spoke.

'Must dash,' she said in a cut-glass English accent. She blew me a kiss as she left.

On my way back, while I was still a hundred yards away from the house, I recognised Victor by the small, perfect circle of his bald pate. It made him look like a monk. 'Friar Fuck', Fynch has been known to call him behind his back, laughing hardest, as usual, at his own jokes. Victor beamed at me as I approached. He was wearing a garland of dried figs like a tribal necklace over a pale seersucker suit. His grin pushed his receding chin downwards so that he resembled a happy hamster.

'If you are not careful, young man, you will get used to this,' he said. 'You won't be able to return to the book trade. But, then again, they say that active life in the open air protects one from prostate cancer, and you are never too young to start worrying about that, are you?'

He was staying 'up the road in Montenegro', where several of his clients kept enormous yachts in the Bay of Kotor. He had some 'insignificant issue' to clarify with Gorsky. Funny how he happened to turn up on the eve of the party, joining the other English men and women who attached themselves to wealthy Russians like oxpecker birds to hippopotami.

'He is around,' Victor said, 'but no one seems to have

set eyes on him. Our friends over there have grown a touch impatient.'

He nodded towards the banker who was still sitting in the same wicker armchair. The orb of the dying sun was slowly drowning in the wide balloon of the cognac glass in front of him. He pretended not to notice Victor. His tan had come on very nicely.

I woke up early to prepare for my journey to London. My suitcase was already packed. I walked down to the beach for one last swim. The air smelled of pine, lavender and tar. The day was promising to be as sunny and as clear as the previous four. I hadn't seen a cloud since I left England. A jug of chilled watermelon juice waited on the table set under a white parasol on the sandy shore of the little bay. The glass next to it was still misted; someone had just taken it out of the freezer. Ice cubes clinked as though they had been stirred a moment ago. The pastries in a basket covered by a gingham cloth were warm. Whoever had laid my breakfast must have been watching me leave the bungalow.

There were pristine copies of the main British and US newspapers – that morning's: colour scans printed out on better quality paper than the original editions. The British covers carried news about the Prime Minister. His dour Scottish face seemed so remote, his concerns about spending so unreal, that the papers could have come from a different historical era altogether.

I swam in the warm water then spread my limbs and allowed my body to float. I thought about the girl from last night. She did not seem like a prostitute to me, not at all, yet, honestly, whenever I entered Gorsky's world I lost my bearings, as though money created its own decompression chambers in which even the laws of gravity ceased to apply.

Human noise muffled by the water in my ears reached me from not so far away. I spotted a jet boat a couple of hundred yards from the shore. The Spaniard was at the steering wheel. He had, ridiculously, two pairs of sunglasses on his head: one perched on his nose, while the other held his hair in place, like an Alice band. He was wearing a fresh snow-white shirt. He looked like a retired footballer, or a Formula One driver, the quintessence of a Latin playboy. He was so macho that he was paradoxically almost feminine. At that extreme, the sexes correspond so closely to each other that they become a narcissistic one, in love with no one but their own image.

The girl I had been puzzling over sat immediately behind him. A tiny neon green bikini covered the now familiar cones of her breasts. Just thinking about them gave me the stirring of an erection. She was facing backwards, playing the spotter for the waterskier who was leaning back on his skis, passing his weight from one foot to another with practised comfort as he turned to signal something to her with his left hand. She raised her fist in the air, showing an ace sign with her thumb. The wetsuit and the sun visor made the man look even more alien than usual but his equine muzzle was unmistakeable.

When I returned to the bungalow, my suitcase had already been whisked away. I left a twenty-pound note under the vase of cornflowers on the side table, but I was not even sure that there was a chambermaid here who would welcome my tip. The house was meticulously cleaned every day; glossy magazines were delivered with baskets of fruit; jugs of fresh orange juice, bottles of champagne and supplies of three kinds of water were replenished in the fridge. When I read two books by John le Carré during my first two days, a further four were added to the library, but I never saw anyone going in or out. There was no one to bid my farewells to.

While I was leaving, facing backwards on the golf buggy which had delivered me four days earlier, I noticed the three Russian women leaving the main house in the direction of the jetty where their boat was already waiting. They waved and blew air kisses in my direction. Their menfolk were nowhere to be seen.

I was a lone traveller in the helicopter as it took off, although I spotted two others coming in to land. They hovered in mid-air like vast birds of prey. I now regretted the soundproofing of our cabin. I would have enjoyed my part in this scene from an oligarch's take on *Apocalypse Now*, yet I could barely hear the sound of the rotor blades above my own head. The incoming machines seemed completely silent. The wistful voice of the pilot startled me. He was speaking to someone on his radio.

'Those are the latest Sikorskys, Bud. Those guys could have a shower onboard if they wanted. The boss is putting on a show. Moscow, you bet.'

The little airport was as deserted as before. The same hostess welcomed me on board with a parting gift, a flacon of home-pressed olive oil as dark as sea kelp. It was delivered in a small wicker case, with a handwritten note. *Hope you had a good rest*, it read, *and we look forward to seeing you again very soon*. The handwriting was girly, the final n ending in an elaborate flourish of black ink. But it was signed in sepia, in a different hand: the jagged and hurried initials RBG, in Russian Cyrillic. The lid of the G trailed upwards like a dagger.

Back in London the drizzle was as persistent as when I left. It was part of the cityscape, as constant as the buildings and the streets. The same solitary border agency official checked my passport. Gorsky's driver helped me get into the car and asked me to wait as he disappeared and returned with a small attaché case which he put on the front seat. Then Gorsky emerged immediately behind him. I am not sure if he was on the same plane. The timing of my private flight did not entirely tally with his waterskiing performance, yet here he was, as though teleported. I was getting used to his antics but, surely, even he wouldn't fly two jets on the same route within minutes of each other. He opened the car door himself. He glanced at my lap – the blue hat tube and the wicker basket with olive oil.

'How was Hesperos?' he asked.

'How does one buy an island like that?' I responded with a question. 'Just curious. I am not thinking of getting one.'

He smiled.

'It came with the Karagiannis portfolio. The ship builder, you remember. In the nineteen nineties I spent much of my time in Sofia. It's a claustrophobic town, and it was even more so before they joined the EU. It's one of those places where having money doesn't help because however much of it you have, there's nothing much to spend it on. You still drive along potholed roads and know that people are living in leaky concrete blocks behind billboards advertising tobacco. I had to escape every now and then. I was trading with Serbia in those days – sanctions busting, you remember? And, whatever anyone says, I wasn't in it for the money. Your people were suffering needlessly and the West . . . well, you know all about it. I had this ideal of *helping people* – what else can you do with your life that makes as much sense?'

I had no idea what he was talking about. Fond though I was of my nation, I had few illusions about my co-nationals. He was clearly spinning a myth out of shady mafia deals. He pulled a slim card-case out of his pocket and showed me a photograph inside its flap: a picture of himself looking younger, next to a woman I recognised as one of my country's most eminent surgeons, a former minister of health. She had famously built one of the most modern children's hospitals in Europe with an anonymous donation. In the picture, she and Gorsky were standing in front of an Orthodox chapel with a distinctive red and yellow façade.

'The Rayevsky memorial chapel in southern Serbia, near the Bulgarian border,' Gorsky explained, 'designed by a Russian architect. Even the saplings for the avenue of lime trees were brought over from the motherland. Remember Vronsky from *Anna Karenina*? Tolstoy used the story of a real man, Count Nikolai Rayevsky, who fought the Turks in Serbia in the eighteen seventies and died there. Vronsky was my kind of hero: one part pan-Slavism; two parts death-wish, if you will. I had a similar story back in Russia. A woman to forget. But instead of dying in battle, I got to deal with old Vassilis Karagiannis and I received Hesperos in part-payment . . .'

I watched the streets of London unfurl past us. I never knew what I was allowed to ask, what was appropriate. We sat like that for a few long minutes.

'Have you ever been married?' I finally ventured.

He turned towards me, threw me a long searching look, and ignored my question. We crossed London in silence, entering it from the east without even noticing, then through the City where huge blocks shone with fully lit windows and no sign of human activity, along a moribund Fleet Street and into the West End where thousands walked, shopped, and spoke and peered into their telephones. We circled around Trafalgar Square, along the Mall, closer and closer to his Tower of Babel.

The Summerscales' windows were dark, although the front lawn was floodlit like a football pitch. Gorsky's palace was beginning to take shape, its late-seventeenth-century self carefully restored, but now wrapped in billowing new curves in a thrilling post-modern dance – one of the most fashionable architects in the world showing off her genius. We came to a stop in front of my gatehouse. The driver was already out and walking around to hold open the door for me when I had the flash of an idea so obvious that it was baffling why it hadn't occurred to me before. Halfway out already, my bottle of oil and my panama hat in my hands, I turned and asked:

'Have you met Natalia Summerscale? She lives opposite. A Russian woman.'

His face froze for a moment.

'Summerscale? I know of no Summerscale. What kind of a name is that?'

Two days later I ran into Gery Pekarova in the same supermarket on the King's Road. Of an evening, the place was full of singletons like us, people unable to plan further than the next meal, carrying single pints of milk to the till. This time, she was pushing a trolley with a large bunch of kale and texting furiously. I half hid behind a display of cereal boxes, trying to decide whether to speak to her or not, but she made a U-turn and pushed straight towards me. She grabbed me by the lapels. Her nails were cut almost to the quick and painted a ridiculous shade of blue. She leaned so close into me that I could feel her faintly sweaty, powdery smell. She planted a big wet kiss on my lips.

'Hey, Nikita, I was just thinking that I can't face shopping tonight. Join me at the Eagle for a salad and a glass of wine. I have a story to tell. I was given a special task, you could say.'

'Natalia?' I asked, suspecting another matchmaking plot. I had been avoiding the Summerscales ever since my strange dinner with Tom Summerscale, Janice and Sally.

'No. Well, yes. It's not her. It's about her. We should have guessed long ago.'

She walked me out of the supermarket, leaving her trolley and the kale in the middle of the store. I dropped my empty basket by the entrance.

Gery started the tale over a plateful of lentils and goat's cheese and ended it in her bed with its view of St Luke's. It kept us going through two hours and two bottles of wine, then a couple of joints in her flat. (She refused cigarettes religiously but always had a small stash of weed hidden behind the protein shakes in her kitchen cupboard.) It took us through love-making and a shared shower in her tiny bathroom. Gery's pubic hair, a mat of tight black curls, was now shaped into a heart. Given the story she was telling, one had to laugh at the idea that it was with an eye to Gorsky that she had commissioned that piece of intimate topiary. I think I mentioned already that I was not a jealous type, and certainly not so in relation to this woman. The idea of Gorsky falling for a detail like that would have been ridiculous long before she suggested that he had apparently been celibate for at least the past five years.

'Oh, you know,' Gery said philosophically, 'it is the celibacy that excites me almost as much as his money. What a bloody waste. But expensive men often turn out to have cheap tastes in the long run. The exact opposite of you, book moth.'

'Book *worm*, you mean.'

'Moth, worm, whatever.' She held the tip of my penis and twisted it clockwise by one hundred and eighty degrees. It was still aching as I walked down the King's Road trying to process the story Gery had told me. Gorsky had shared it with her precisely so that she could ask me a favour, a silly and childish favour, like a plot people might get involved in on the teenage dating scene, or so it would have been but for the complexity and costliness of its proposed execution.

When he was sacked from his university post, Gorsky briefly traded in Chinese toys – buying in China, selling in Russia – working with a Chinese man he had studied with at Leningrad. But toys were boring: a small-time training ground. His move into the Balkans was encouraged by the legendary mayor of Volgograd, Nikolai Semyonovich Volkov, recently retired but still living in the town, and well connected everywhere from East Berlin to Shanghai. And still a Communist, a true believer. He had no interest in money, but every interest in stopping the seemingly unstoppable, the spread of NATO to the borders of Russia itself. Just how Gorsky was selected remains unclear. His Chinese links might have helped. He was invited to Volgograd. He became, for a while, Volkov's sixth child. He may well have been a substitute son. Volkov's eldest, Sergey, was killed in Afghanistan in the eighties. He met – befriended – his adoptive siblings; the middle three. The youngest, Natalia, was away from home, reading for an art history degree in what was now again St Petersburg. Gorsky was twelve years older than her. He was too old to be love-struck, yet love-struck he was, the moment he set eyes on her baccalaureate photograph. She was still in her school uniform. A *coup de foudre*, Gery said. He was a monomaniac in love as in everything else. He had to have her.

Natalia turned up in Volgograd trailing stories of museums and white nights on the Neva and looking even more beautiful than her picture. Gorsky was so determined to marry her that he spoke to her father long before he had spoken to her. She must have encouraged him, nonetheless. One evening, he dropped on a bended knee and produced a small box out of his top pocket. Natalia pushed it away with her hand, trying to prevent the inevitable opening and whispered, 'No, I can't, I am too young.'

No, I can't.

He wouldn't take no for an answer. Gery had no idea what exactly Natalia promised, but Gorsky had no doubt that she had left an opening, that she would eventually be his. He would wait. He would make money. He would work and he would wait. He loved her even more because she had turned him down. He promised her that he would return when she graduated and propose again.

And so he did, he told Gery. He kept his word. He returned to Volgograd some three years later only to find that, according to his interpretation of their agreement, she hadn't kept hers, that she had married an Englishman and left the country. He was so convinced that she was in love with him, and him alone, that the Englishman was nothing but a convenient passport, that he decided to make his millions and offer her another chance to be his wife.

'Why do you think he is building that place? He thinks that one day soon, when it's all ready, she will just cross the road, leave Summerscale behind like one leaves a restaurant after a pleasant meal, and be his.

'In fact, he wants you to arrange a meeting in your little bookshop, in exactly two weeks' time. The anniversary of his original proposal. She was nineteen when they first met, she is thirty now,' Gery said, 'but she is as beautiful as ever and he loves her as much as that first day.'

What Gorsky did not know – what nobody knew except Natalia and Gery; and Gery was now telling me – is that she had loved him for the last nine out of those eleven years, without any plan ever to become his wife. They had another encounter when she was twenty-one, a meeting he had neglected to mention when he told his story to Gery. Natalia had been on the books of an escort agency in St Petersburg for several months when it happened. In those murky days, the city's cafes were full of pimps pretending to be scouts for modelling agencies, and a young woman as beautiful as Natalia was an obvious target. Out of rebellion, out of her own thirst for experience and money, but at first simply because she was naive, she accepted engagements in expensive hotels.

'Don't look so shocked, Nikita,' Gery said. 'I am not a complete stranger to the business myself. When powerful men stop buying sex, powerful women will stop selling it. I have never been sure precisely, but I think she met Tom on an assignment too. What is the exact difference between selling your body and marrying for money? Anyway, she had one rule: that her clients must be foreign, not Russian. She hardly wanted some crusty old friend of her dad turning up. One night, someone made a mistake. She was called to a hotel room expecting an Israeli businessman celebrating an arms deal. The concierge had already sent a bottle of vintage Dom Perignon to the room. When the door opened, she saw Gorsky.'

I took a deep breath to say something and stayed like that.

'What did he do?' Gery supplied the question. 'He said absolutely nothing, asked no questions. And she? She did her job. She left his room with ten thousand dollars, in love, and convinced that he would never want to see her again.'

'You must be joking,' I finally reacted. 'You must be bloody joking. I can't believe a single word you are saying. You are the last person I'd have expected to fall for such sentimental rubbish, Gergana. Men who make that much money are brutal, they don't fall in love like that. Women who work as escorts and marry people like Tom Summerscale don't pine in secret for some long-lost Prince Charming.'

'You know nothing,' Gery said. 'Money has nothing to do with anything. You make very little money, you feel very little, you are fine. You are a bolter, Nikola, aren't you? And you fancy Natalia because it's a form of running away: like being infatuated with a Hollywood star, pinning her pictures on the wall. But you should do this for Roman Gorsky. He pays your rent.'

I wondered how to engineer an invitation to Natalia Summerscale. I knew something about her husband that Gorsky would no doubt love to hear, but I did not want to be part of any sordid revenge plot. My walk home was at an end and my head was buzzing with this new spin on the world I had inadvertently entered and was – I thought – just beginning to understand. I wondered if Gorsky had planned it all, exactly as it was unfolding, long before I met him, long before he entered Fynch's that first time.

I stood between The Laurels and the Barracks, one beautifully lit, the other still a builder's take on Passchendaele, with a dome suspended in mid-air. As I now knew, it was a Taj Mahal for the living, a monument to human folly if there ever was one, but one already emerging in its promised ethereal beauty.

6

Я помню чудное мгновенье:
Передо мной явилась Ты,
Как мимолетное виденье,
Как гений чистой красоты.

A magic moment I remember:
I raised my eyes and you were there,
A fleeting vision, the quintessence
Of all that's beautiful and rare

A. S. Pushkin—

The following day Christopher Fynch received a call from one of the most fashionable interior designers in London. The man expressed a burning desire to put aside his work on a major restaurant opening in Covent Garden and drop by, to organise, absolutely free of charge, a few 'makeover touches' to our shop. Fynch did not believe a word of it: who would? He persisted in thinking it was an elaborate scam, even when the man offered to send over his two assistants to take some photographs that same afternoon. Only when a couple of black-clad, sharp-suited women stepped out of a taxi and started measuring and taking pictures did Fynch begin to panic. He looked at the untidy piles that perched precariously everywhere, at the messy yards of shelving upon which lay books that had never been returned to their proper place once a careless reader took them to another section or dropped them on another pile. There were pleasant little nooks with chairs that should have been reupholstered decades ago, there were many places where shelves were held in place by books rather than the other way round, there were notices for concerts by long-dead musicians, charity auctions for abandoned causes, flyers advertising out-of-print titles.

Fynch did not want anything changed. More to the point, he couldn't afford to change anything. The women assured him that he wasn't expected to pay a penny. A benefactor had given their famous boss a blank cheque. His only condition was to be able to hold a private event, a book launch or a *vernissage*, perhaps, for a small, very select audience. He was ready to pay any reasonable sum Fynch would care to ask for to have the sole use of the bookshop for a couple of hours.

I turned up for my shift while they were explaining the brief. I had a pretty good idea of the identity of the anonymous patron. I was not surprised to hear that Gorsky had been setting things in motion even before I had consented to the plan that Gery had described. No sooner had I mentioned Gorsky than Fynch changed his tune: of course the shop was beautiful and unique and precious exactly as it was, but if someone would – could – rewire and re-plumb, and sort out some new shelving, a few new leather armchairs, and a new desk with perhaps a functioning computer terminal so that we could know what we have in stock and where . . . and a better security system, cameras perhaps, and, yes, some mirrors . . . Oh, and a final small thing, but not an unimportant one, a new loo downstairs, just in case the guests at the launch

. . . But how could it all be done – he wrung his hands with anxiety – in such a short time and without major loss of trade?

Even at the highest possible estimate, the amount of trade lost for each of the five days that the bookshop remained closed was such that Gorsky must have found the sum laughable. Fynch laughed too, all the way to Northumberland, where he spent the week with long-lost friends while I volunteered to keep an eye on the business of redecoration. It was impossible to believe that the bookshop would be dismantled completely and then put back together – just as it was, only better, they promised – in five days, but this is precisely what Mr Famous Interior Decorator had guaranteed. This was as much time as he could spare from his commission in Covent Garden without endangering progress there. This was as long as Gorsky could afford to wait: for someone who had waited more than ten years he was now getting rather impatient. I couldn't follow his logic – what exactly was the problem with the old Fynch's? The love of his life grew up in

Stalingrad, she must have seen places much worse than our temple to genteel shabbiness.

Whatever the problem with the old bookshop might have been, the new one looked the same but a million times better – a Hollywood take on shabby gentility, a bookshop that could have featured George Clooney and Anthony Hopkins as me and Christopher Fynch. Our books were in perfect order on shelves that practically shone with high polish. The precious wood reflected my face from every corner; antique mirrors caught it and multiplied it in mellow amber light. In hidden nooks, deep armchairs smelled of expensive leather. Even our old signs – fiction, biography, travel, poetry – were remade in tarnished gold plate, copying Fynch's own handwriting. Most unbelievable of all, deep in the bowels of the shop, was the new art history section.

It now housed the entire conceptualist collection that I had gradually amassed to attract the custom of Natalia Summerscale. Where the rest of the bookshop was fitted in mahogany and morocco leather against an eau de Nil wallpaper, here everything was honeyed. The walls between the rosewood shelves were covered with backlit amber panels. An armchair and a sofa facing it were upholstered in golden velvet. On small side tables, three golden bowls held bonsai mimosa trees in full bloom. Their discreet powdery smell brought to mind late February in the Adriatic, the coming of spring, a promise of renewal, not a miserable afternoon in London, in a year in which most days seemed to belong to some never-ending late November. Was this even possible? I asked myself stupidly, again and again.

I was as nervous as a teenage bridegroom when Gery rang to confirm that Natalia was happy to come to tea at Fynch's to view my new art department. We had to finish by six. She was going to see Daisy in a school play and she wouldn't miss that for the world.

I may have been nervous, but I was not half as nervous as Gorsky seemed to be when he appeared, almost an hour ahead of the appointed time, to ensure that everything was as he wanted it and that the shop was closed to all other customers. There had been, by our standards, surprising numbers ever since the word of our flash-redecoration spread to the rich, riparian hinterland of our customer-base, stretching westwards along the lush banks of the Thames from Chelsea to Chiswick and Richmond and Kew. Gorsky paced about half-listening, shooting restless glances here and there. At one point, to draw his attention, I started a sentence with 'Mr Gorsky'. He turned abruptly yet it was evident that something in him had already melted:

'Nikolai, please, enough with formality. Roman, please . . .'

He grabbed my arms with both hands as if to steady himself. We walked up to the sales desk where he personally tested the functioning of our new security system as though he was worried that Natalia might try to assassinate him. I had to show him how to train the camera in the arts section several times.

'Are you sure that it is recording?' he asked. I paused and rewound a bit of film which showed the empty set, the dwarf mimosa trees, the glow of amber panels. He seemed pleased with what he saw. He stared into the screen, looking into the emptiness of the room as though he was trying to look into his own future. He was dressed as impeccably as ever in a charcoal suit and a white shirt, with a silk tie in a rich lilac grey. He seemed at once much older and much younger than usual. I raised a hand to remove a white speck of paper from his sleeve and he flinched as though I was about to hit him.

Finally, he went downstairs. I watched him through the eye of the security camera. Every sign of restlessness slowly drained away. He straightened his jacket, took an armchair, crossed his right leg over his left and waited.

She was half an hour late. She took me aback by coming on foot, breathless and apologetic, her coat over her arm, wearing a shirt of golden silk over a pair of green velvet trousers, as though she had had some advance idea of the colour scheme of the space that had been so carefully prepared for her. Under a coiffed chignon, several locks of golden hair were escaping studiedly towards the vertebrae of her long neck. She looked around herself in wonderment.

'You have had a refit? This is lovely. Absolutely lovely.'

'And wait till you see the art section,' I said, suddenly

scared as I guided her towards the back of the shop. When we were about to turn into the amber room, I seized her by the elbow, wanting to forewarn her, but I had no idea whether to tell her to run inside or away.

I saw Gorsky stand up from his armchair and take a step towards her. She looked back at me for less than a split second, startled, then gave a little animal squeal. I followed her in, but she turned towards me and dismissed me with a single flick of her hand.

It started raining. For the next half an hour I stared at the security screen under the desk while trying not to look. Whereas before we hardly cared if someone tried to steal a book, we now had the most discreet and sophisticated CCTV system in existence. For all Fynch and I knew, the shop was bugged to the gills too: all for this one meeting. It was difficult to guess the mood of the conversation. If his face was expressionless, hers was even more so. Finally Gorsky stood up and then she did, and they walked towards each other and he held her for several long moments. Then they walked out of the room.

When they reached the till where I was sitting, pretending

to enter some data into the swish new computer system, Natalia looked happier than I had ever seen her before. It might be more correct to say that she looked happy for the first time. Gorsky was speaking into his mobile phone.

'I'd like you at the site as soon as possible, please,' he was saying, although his *please* sounded as though it left no room for manoeuvre. 'I am sure that the trustees will understand that you can't always present the bid in person. This is more important.'

I could not hear what was important because Natalia was speaking to me.

'Dearest Nicholas, I am so glad to have come here today. Would you be able to accompany us? Roman tells me it's by your house anyway. I had no idea you lived so close. Roman wants to show me the exhibition space he is creating. It will take forty-five minutes at most. I have to be at Daisy's school at six. I need to have your company, please . . .'

I grabbed my coat and prepared to lock up the shop.

By the time we reached the Barracks, Gorsky's architect was there and waiting. You couldn't fail to recognise the woman. There are few architects who regularly appear on the covers of glossy fashion magazines and whose image is as well known as their work. She was like some small bird, tiny and dressed head to toe in black clothes that were themselves architectural rather than tailored. Her hair was black too, and startlingly shiny, but for a single thick white strand tucked behind her left ear. Her lips were covered in brightest red lipstick, and her forced smile made them look like a gash. Her English had an East Coast American twang.

'Xiulan Xi,' she introduced herself needlessly and shook Natalia's hand, then mine.

'Delighted to meet you,' Natalia responded without giving her own name.

'Nikola Kimovic,' I said, feeling more than slightly stupid. I might have said 'Horton the Elephant' for all the attention she paid.

'I am sorry to have taken you away from your work at such short notice,' Gorsky said to the woman. 'However, I am sure that the trustees of the V&A can reach their decision on the basis of your drawings, not your presence.'

Only her red lips smiled. She took the three of us straight to the dome. Even at ground level, the vantage point provided amazing views south across the Thames, and north towards The Laurels and the rest of Chelsea. By the time the cantilevered viewing platform, hidden inside the dome, was completed, the owner would have the whole of London – from Crystal Palace to Harrow – on the palm of their hand. Alternatively, if they preferred to stay inside, they would be able to view some of the finest European baroque fresco painting from as close as it was last seen by the painter himself.

If Natalia looked happy when she left Fynch's she now seemed transported. Her face was half hidden by the hood of her coat, lined with some amber fur. Gorsky looked neither at the architect nor at the astonishing project she was describing, and he certainly did not look at me. He stared at Natalia's face as though bewitched. If I hadn't been jealous, I might have found it almost funny. And I was indescribably, immeasurably jealous. Not of the idea, which now seemed certain, that he might soon have this woman for ever, not of the building nor of the money he possessed, but of his capacity to feel.

The stereotypical compensatory story would run along these lines: I may be earning a little more than the minimum wage but at least I have friends and family and real feelings, real love. I wish. I may not have been one of Camus' sociopathic anti-heroes, but years ago I had somehow cut myself from the kind of feeling I was now witnessing. I had assumed that my entire generation was like that. We refused the war – we refused the world – by disengaging. We got stoned or fucked or drank ourselves to oblivion. This man was breaking the cardinal rule. He was in love.

I lost the thread of Xiulan Xi's presentation as I followed the three of them through what had been the grand dining room with its newly installed modern loggias made of billowing glass and steel, like silk falling out of gashes in the sleeves of renaissance costumes. It was clearly the work of a genius who respected the old but wasn't frightened of taking risks with it. I could see why Gorsky selected her when he could have had Gehry, Hadid, Piano or Calatrava. She had a lot in common with all of them but there was also something about her design that made her work – almost – Russian.

The architect was now explaining the many ways in which she had responded to her client's brief: to create one of the largest and grandest exhibition spaces in London. The Turbine Hall at Tate Modern might be larger, she conceded, but it displays much less and it is nowhere near as impressive as what you would see here – and what you will see more clearly when the space is finished. All it needs is an art collection to showcase: be it an installation or an old-fashioned sculpture, this space will display art at its best through flattery rather than rivalry.

When she rushed ahead to show us how the loggias could be adjusted to different specifications, Gorsky glanced at me for the first time.

'Do you possess a large art collection?' I asked.

'No,' he said, 'only a couple of small Chagalls. But

I am about to start acquiring more. I will soon have a curator to help me.'

At that, Natalia beamed.

When Xiulan Xi finished her guided tour, it was Natalia who invited Gorsky and me to the play.

'You boys might never get another chance to see *The Lion, the Witch and the Wardrobe* performed by a bunch of English school kids,' she said.

Gorsky accepted instantly and enthusiastically. Hearing him being called a boy was only marginally less strange than the idea of seeing him in the audience at a pre-prep school. When Natalia suggested that we would be less conspicuous if we took a black cab, he immediately offered his car and driver to Xiulan Xi, and stepped into the street to summon a taxi with a loud whistle.

Something about the way he perched on its seat suggested that he was less familiar with London taxis than even I was. He studied the interior with curiosity and observed in Russian that it reminded him of his student days. This was probably his idea of roughing it for her sake. I sat on a fold-out seat facing them and feeling vaguely ridiculous, like a Victorian chaperone, while he furtively held her hand throughout the short journey. I observed his bodyguards catching up on motorcycles, then following the taxi in a discreet, impromptu cavalcade.

Daisy's school was housed in a large Gothic villa on the south side of Hyde Park. Although it looked like a place dreamed up by J. K. Rowling, it was clear – in spite of Natalia's promise of a 'bunch of English school kids' – that its pupils were the offspring of international billionaires; perhaps means-tested scholarships were on offer to the children of mere multi-millionaires. Its theatre may have looked like a scaled-down version of the English National Opera, but the audience was anything but English. There were Indians, Arabs, Chinese, Americans, Germans, and even a few Russian women. On seeing Gorsky, who studiedly remained closer to me than to Natalia, they immediately stopped talking to each other and tried to secure seats nearer us. The air was thick with expensive scents and all the women present were dressed in ostentatious and very un-English ways. Their fur coats, shiny handbags, high heels and multiple rings with huge stones made Natalia's silk shirt and velvet trousers seem modest, and her chignon positively understated. The only couple whose Englishness I could be certain of was a Premier League footballer and his wife, who was more famous than him, though I wasn't sure exactly why. I noticed in the glossy brochure that their six-year-old son – with a ridiculously non-English name – was about to play Aslan.

As the heiress to her mother's blonde looks, Daisy was destined to play the White Witch. Although her voice still had its childish pitch, she delivered her lines with the poise of the young Queen Elizabeth. All the children spoke with pukka English accents. If you ignored the multitude of races on stage, the performance was positively Edwardian. The teachers, who dressed and sounded like Oxbridge graduates, fluttered about – giving whispered instructions to the orchestra, moving antique furniture on stage, making sure that the elaborate costumes did not trip up the little performers. When the play ended, they led the tumultuous applause, which lasted several minutes.

I noticed that the Russian women, having manoeuvred themselves alongside us, kept looking at Gorsky as intently as they looked at their sons and daughters on stage. When everyone finally stood up, they moved towards Natalia with great urgency and each kissed her on the cheeks three times in the Orthodox fashion, asking about her health in high-pitched, excitable Russian. When one asked after Tom Summerscale, Gorsky winced. As they preened themselves and waited to be introduced, they clearly did not care if Natalia was stepping out with Gorsky, deceiving her husband or playing some other, more complicated game. Roman Gorsky was the most eligible man in the world: if he could be touched, he could be stolen. Even before Gery materialised from somewhere, with the little White Witch in tow, they were inviting him to their parties, handing out their cards from slim golden boxes, going about their pursuits as elegantly as the courtesans at Versailles.

Throughout it all, Gorsky displayed barely a flicker of interest. He stared around discourteously, nodding but not listening. When the little girl appeared, her face beneath a sparkling tiara still covered in silvery white powder, he was transformed in an instant. He focused on her expression so completely that the little witch could have touched him with her wand. He barely registered Natalia's introduction, or heard her as she urged her daughter to shake 'Uncle Roman's hand'.

The child curtseyed and looked at him. Their faces spread into instantaneous wide smiles.

'How old are you, little princess?' Gorsky asked.

'Five and three-quarters. Almost six,' she responded.

She raised her arms towards him and he lifted her as high as he could, then lowered her just enough to bury his head into the multiple tulle layers of her skirt. Natalia looked at Gery, and Gery looked at me, as though we were all witnessing some kind of miracle.

'You are not needed any more,' Gery whispered in my ear as she pulled me away. 'Summerscale never attends these plays anyway, but he had to fly to Zurich this afternoon. He won't be back until tomorrow night. I have just told Natalia. Shall we push the boat out and go for a bite somewhere? Let's find somewhere normal. A pizza place perhaps? Is there one around here? The three of them are walking, by the way. This is a day of miracles.'

Her face spread into a broad, simian smile.

I turned her invitation down. My head was throbbing. Images of the day kept running through it like a bewildering film reel: the security screens at Fynch's showing that extraordinary embrace when Gorsky held Natalia without so much as attempting to kiss her; Xiulan Xi; the very Anglican magic of the play in contrast with the sheer foreignness of its audience; most of all, perhaps, those Russian women whose eyes so plainly shone as they responded to the naked attraction of Gorsky's money. It was as though his capital created a kind of vortex around him. He luxuriated in the silent centre where the ozone pooled, while all around him people fainted with breathlessness and greed.

I longed to escape into something very English and rural, the world which existed on this island before any of us new immigrants had England in our sights: ancient oak forests, valleys full of sheep, the aboriginal population of mean country squires and miserable farmhands, cold little churches with mouldy prayer books and the tattered flags of county regiments; an empty, empty world. I was trying so hard to think of a novel by Thomas Hardy that I hadn't read, that I felt tempted to dive into Fynch's and check our now highly organised shelves. Yet the shop too was swept up in Gorsky's vortex. The footfall increased, the sales rocketed, and we featured in a couple of glossy supplements as one of London's most romantic 'secret spots' just as we became anything but secret. I actually preferred the old shop. It would take years before this glossy new thing even began to resemble it. I thought of Gorsky throwing insane amounts of money about and wished he had thrown them back at villages in Russia.

I unlocked the door of my little dwelling, which Gorsky now owned. I made a cup of camomile tea, fished out a battered copy of *Jude the Obscure* and prepared to retire to bed. As I drew the curtains, I tried not to look towards the Barracks. Instead, I went over to the other set of windows. The lawn in front of The Laurels was lit so brightly that my ceiling was bathed in a greenish reflected light, even across two lanes of traffic. In the middle of it stood Natalia and Gorsky, kissing.

This day was the beginning of something he had planned for over a decade, with the precision of a field marshal. But what if what had been driving him was not Natalia but her refusal?

7

I was startled out of my morning reading by a ring on the door. The woman introduced herself as Siobhan MacDonald. Her soft Irish accent, her name and her tired face under a messy pile of grey hair were vaguely familiar. She was once the BBC's Moscow correspondent, she said. Now freelance, she was working on a series of articles for one of those mid-market dailies I have never even opened. 'My Russian Neighbours' was the running title. I was living next door to the most famous yet most elusive Russian of them all.

She explained all this while standing on my doorstep. Behind her, passing buses and cars threw up sprays of muddy drops and a soft mist. It was difficult to decide whether it was raining or not, and just as difficult to decide whether or not to invite her in. Something about her little black ballerina shoes, completely wrong both for her age and for the weather, made me take pity on her.

'Have you ever met Roman Gorsky?' She came straight to the point the moment she made herself comfortable in my tiny living room with the cup of tea I had offered and prepared.

'Not really,' I said.

'What he's doing here is that he's transforming the Chelsea Yeomanry Barracks, a grade-one listed building and one of the most important monuments of the English baroque, into a private palace. Are you aware that he had obtained planning permission by promising to convert a substantial portion into a public space? There are rumours that he was acting under false pretences, that he is already going back on that promise.'

'Should I be worried?' I asked.

'I don't know. Should you? He is digging four storeys below ground as though owning what is already the largest residential building in London is not enough. Doesn't all this work disturb you, living next door, as you do? On top of it, you could say?' Her eyes followed the length of one of the wider fissures in my walls.

'Not really. I am never at home. I work all day.'

'And at weekends?'

'At weekends, too.'

'It's not just the ordinary stuff, if you could call any of it ordinary,' she continued, 'Walk-in wardrobes, swimming pools, gyms, garages, kitchens that would put the Savoy to shame, a private cinema . . . even – I hear – a hairdresser's. Why would a man who lives alone need his own hairdressing salon, for heaven's sake? It's also the insane levels of security. Not a panic room but a panic apartment three storeys below ground, with its own escape tunnel to the Thames embankment, they say. All the windows bullet proofed, air purifiers throughout – and not because your Mr Gorsky fears hay fever.'

'Honestly,' I interrupted, 'If the man fears a gas attack, or wants his hair done daily, let him have what he wants.

This sort of thing keeps the British economy going. It's not as though it's any of our business.'

'They keep complaining about the lack of housing in London. Yet he also owns a flat in the Barbican,' she said. 'A former bishop's palace just outside London. A castle in Scotland. A villa on Rublevka, half a mile from Putin's, valued at thirty million pounds. A chalet in Switzerland. An entire island in Greece. Isn't it strange to want so much space?'

'Money needs space, I guess. This doesn't trouble me. If it did, I'd try to earn more than I do.'

'And how much is that?'

She took a photograph. I named the sum. Fynch had instructed me to give myself a pay rise appropriate for my new tasks, but I hadn't bothered to do so. I couldn't face explaining it now.

Her article, when it appeared some days later in a newspaper owned by another Russian billionaire, had a picture of me, smiling, a chipped enamel mug in my hands, on a tatty sofa with piles of books and papers all around me and a view of several large cranes in the window behind. The caption read: '*Slav labour.*'

The piece misspelled my name: 'Nick Himovic (38), a refugee from the war-torn Balkans, lives in the shadow of Roman Gorsky's project. He says the massive building work is "no trouble". He spends every waking hour working on the shop floor and he earns less than the minimum wage. He has never met his wealthy next-door neighbour.'

In the foreground, you could see my big toe, protruding from a large hole in my sock, just above the edge of the coffee table on which lay opened a newspaper on the page that I had been reading, quite coincidentally, when she rang the bell, and which featured a large – and totally untypical – picture of Gorsky in a skull cup. Its graininess suggested a wide lens and a great distance. She had a better eye than I, Ms MacDonald. It could have been worse. I could have told her that I was to be evicted the moment Gorsky moved in.

Her portrait of Gorsky, which featured my cameo appearance, was presented as a classic tale of rags to riches. Gorsky was born wretchedly poor in a shared apartment in one of those Dickensian warrens within Leningrad's dilapidated palaces which smelled of sewage, coal and pickle whatever the season. His father, Boris Moiseevich

Gorsky, a printer, died of throat cancer when the boy was seven. His mother, Elizaveta Alexandrovna Stern, had worked as a guard at the Hermitage well into the 1990s, even as her son made his first billions. She was one of those babushkas who knew more about art than you would guess from their uniforms. Elizaveta's brother, Isaac Stern, a chess player, got his nephew interested in mathematics. It was Isaac, through his contacts in the world of international chess, who got Gorsky to Basel for a month when he was a student, a visit that opened his eyes to the riches of the West. Gorsky was typical of that generation of young Russian entrepreneurs who benefited from Yeltsin's reforms and the murky waters of economic restructuring in the early 1990s: driven, ruthless, possibly murderous. Why would he care about some small Serbian guy next door when he did not care about anyone? He lived alone. His God was Greed.

Whether the PR effort at establishing good neighbourly relations had anything to do with my interview or not, a few days after the piece appeared I was alarmed to see

Tom Summerscale and a small group of elderly citizens of Chelsea standing by my front door, about to embark on a tour of the Barracks. They were led by Xiulan Xi and – most astonishingly – Gorsky himself, escorted not so discreetly by a couple of his bodyguards and three young women who handed out leaflets about fresco conservation and the community benefits of eco-friendly urban garden design.

I hadn't seen the boys – his *malchiki* – for a while. One of them walked over to me and said, in a soft Russian-inflected voice that left no space for refusal, 'Mr Gorsky asks if you would like to join us, please to join us . . .' Gorsky gave me a tight-lipped little nod. The architect showed no sign of recognising me. Summerscale slapped me on the back and made me cough. I wondered if he had any idea about Natalia's renewed acquaintance with our neighbour.

'I think you will find the sense of community greatly enhanced by this new space, which Mr Gorsky is planning to open to the public to present not only the best in Russian art but in British and European art too. It will be an asset to the whole of London. Mr Gorsky is known to be one of the leading philanthropists in the world . . .'

Gorsky stared ahead as though Xiulan Xi's speech had nothing to do with him. Summerscale smirked visibly. The architect soldiered on, explaining the highlights of her project and talking about community spirit as though Gorsky was building a gallery for the British nation and not a house for himself, yet all the while she was taking extreme care to emphasise that the project did not involve bringing 'the wrong sort of people' into the area. Her tour came to an end with what amounted to an implicit pitch for her own practice. No project was too small, apparently, for XX Associates (for a moment I thought she said 'Excess Associates'). They created some ingenious adjustments to existing buildings for as little as two million pounds. Summerscale took her card before she marched off towards the waiting cab.

One of the elderly couples – white haired, polite, and as English as they come – walked over to Gorsky just as Summerscale was making a crude comment in Russian about Xiulan Xi, addressing no one in particular. The bodyguards smirked. Summerscale's Russian was accented but fluent. It was difficult to imagine why he was on the tour. I assumed that his path must have crossed Gorsky's long ago and much further east.

'Dear Mr Gorsky, thank you so much for inviting us. This was absolutely fascinating. If you are not in a hurry, it would be lovely if you could join us for tea with Mr Summerscale.'

At that they turned to Summerscale.

'Sir Michael and Lady Leighton,' Gorsky reluctantly introduced the couple: it was clear that Summerscale had no idea who they were, although they evidently knew him.

'Daphne, please,' the woman chipped in.

The couple were dressed in identical green cagoule jackets, with identical green galoshes on their feet. Under her jacket, Daphne wore a black jumper covered in what could have been specks of white angora wool or cat's hair. Sir Michael's frayed regimental tie said little to me, or indeed Gorsky, I guess. Summerscale probably knew how to read the stripes.

The couple spoke in unison, finishing each other's sentences.

'So wonderful to meet you at long last. We were thrilled to hear that you were moving into the neighbourhood a couple of years ago. We knew your father very well. And, dare we say, your father-in-law, Reverend Hugo Leatherdale.'

At that, Gorsky took a step closer, suddenly interested in the conversation. Summerscale raised his left hand, as if to stop their next sentence. His signet ring caught the sunlight.

'My *former* father-in-law . . .'

'Oh dear.' Daphne let out a nervous giggle. 'We do apologise. We didn't realise.'

It did not look as though she had meant it.

'A cup of tea would be most excellent.' Gorsky startled everyone, including the Leightons. He turned to Summerscale.

'Would you care to join us?'

Summerscale walked on with them, perhaps not wanting to be left out of the conversation.

One of the bodyguards gave me a brief nod before he followed the group. No one else said goodbye. My apologies to Gorsky had to wait.

The tea party must have been a success for, some weeks later, Fynch received an invitation to dinner at one of the fashionable new Indian restaurants in Mayfair. *C. F. G. Fynch Esq., and companion*, the invitation said. I wasn't sure how angry Gorsky was after my minute of media fame, but Fynch insisted that I should play the 'companion' and try to mend bridges. He was worried about the future of our library commission: even I was, I admit, particularly now that my services as a Russian Cupid had become redundant. So I went along. The choice of cuisine must have been influenced by the preferences of Gorsky's new acquaintances, for his would have been sushi or caviar. The meal was to be followed by a charity auction for the benefit of Lady Leighton's Donkey Sanctuary on Exmoor. The brochure stated that every item to be auctioned had been donated by Gorsky – and each one, from medieval miniatures with Christmas scenes to pieces of Meissen porcelain and Lalique glass, would feature a donkey.

I was not surprised when one of Gorsky's many assistants called to instruct me to procure as many rare editions of works that included notable literary donkeys as I could lay my hands on at short notice. As I chased signed copies of *Winnie the Pooh* and illustrated versions of *A Midsummer Night's Dream*, I wondered if the whole event had been dreamed up by Gorsky as some kind of coded *fuck-you* for my interview with Siobhan MacDonald. In spite of my protestations of innocence, even Fynch had it pinned on our noticeboard in a rare act of implicit protest. He did not say a thing. When I tried to apologise, he laughed it off but I was sure that the bit about the minimum wage hurt. I don't think he paid himself a salary: before Gorsky arrived, the shop had been operating at a loss for over a decade.

I dreaded the evening. I had no desire to go, and I had a bad feeling about every possible outcome of a situation that would put Gorsky and Summerscale in the same room with Natalia for several hours. However, I had little choice but to get into my hired outfit and jump on a bus to Piccadilly. As I gazed at the London streets through the misted windows on the upper deck, I reflected how a few months, or even a few weeks ago, Gorsky would have sent a car for me. I did not think I was forgotten or even unforgiven, I was simply not needed any more. There was nothing personal about this. His generosity towards our business continued, although – having spent so many of his £250,000 cheques – even I was beginning to think that his library was as big as it ever needed to be.

I was seated at one of the outer tables in the room, with Fynch, his friend Victor, Gery, a buxom Swedish friend of hers who was a receptionist at an indoor tennis club in Fulham, and a taciturn elderly Russian woman who had once worked as a translator for the BBC World Service. She was dressed in a black beaded dress that had seen better days, and a baby-pink bolero made of terry cloth. Victor started flirting with the Swede while we were still examining the noticeboard with the seating arrangements. Fynch tried to talk to the Russian, less out of interest than out of politeness, but gave up halfway through the hors d'oeuvres, although her English was perfect. She spoke with long gasping pauses between words as if to underline the importance of her utterances, yet expressed only absolute banalities, as though she was worried that someone was taping her.

Although we kept smiling at each other, Gery and I had little conversation. She was now hopeful about the way things were unfolding between Natalia and Gorsky but could neither whisper nor say much within ear-shot of so many others, and yet she did not seem to want to talk about much else. She was hoping that any 'transfer' (the word she used to refer to the expected developments, as though Natalia was a footballer) would apply to her as well.

'Tom is a decent guy, and wealthy enough,' she whispered, 'but it's not the sort of wealth that can last, particularly if he stays on in Britain doing nothing as seems to be the case so often nowadays . . . He is trying to live off his property portfolio, and . . . you know . . . there are perils in practically retiring in your mid-forties if you own hundreds of millions, not billions . . . You have too much time on your hands and you start depending on people you don't like.'

She pressed a nostril with an index finger conspiratorially. Victor looked at her, chortled, and – clearly misunderstanding – patted his breast pocket and winked. Soon enough, she disappeared outside with him and the Swede. The Russian woman smiled at me. Fynch was deeply immersed in reading the mottled label on the wine bottle.

At the table in the centre of the room, under an elaborate bower that was supposed to represent *A Midsummer Night's Dream*, the Leightons were resplendent in their antique finery. One would barely have recognised them. Lady Daphne's tiara, atop her white, now carefully curled hair, was like something out of *The Merry Widow*. Next to her sat Gorsky, his face and his poise oddly matching the Leightons' late-Victorian charm. In his tailored dinner jacket, Summerscale looked even more like a rugby player than in his usual day clothes. Natalia was in a white silk dress, with a garland of white silk flowers instead of a boa across her shoulders. As usual, she wore no jewellery. When she spotted me, she waved and threw me a big warm smile, the kind I first saw on her face after her meeting with Gorsky. Next to her, on an embroidered booster cushion, sat Daisy, dressed as Peaseblossom, holding a magic wand. The only child in the huge dining room, she seemed to be enjoying the evening more than anyone else.

Victor had kept his promise to 'bring the girls back before the puddings' and was giggling with them at what he called the naughty end of the table. At our end, Fynch was explaining the ins and outs of a small order placed by someone called Roderick Montgomery-Chadwyck as an illustration of the minor travails of bookselling. The books had been posted the previous week and now seemed to be lost somewhere between London and Windermere. Montgomery-Chadwyck had telephoned the shop that morning requesting a full refund and refusing to wait a day longer. Fynch thought the fellow unreasonable. The Russian woman listened intently and nodded in apparent sympathy.

While the guests consumed white rose petal and Indian pink pepper sorbet between their main course and their pudding, Summerscale, looking flushed with drink, came over to say hello to Victor, who stood up and hugged him like a long-lost friend. Victor introduced the Swede. Summerscale immediately pulled up a chair between them and started flirting with her. Gery laughed encouragingly. She was leaning so close to Victor by this stage that his arm was practically lodged between her breasts. Fynch and the Russian woman had finished their sorbets and were now perusing the auction catalogue most attentively, although it was unlikely that either was going to bid for anything. Perhaps because I kept trying to avoid Summerscale's insistent gaze, he addressed me directly.

'Young Serb,' he said (like everyone else, he had clearly read my unfortunate interview), 'have you forgotten us? You used to drop by to see my lady wife and our lovely friend Gery here; now we hardly ever see you . . . Have you three little Slavs fallen out with each other, or do you perhaps still come when I am not around?' He let out a vulgar throaty laugh.

'I wouldn't worry about Nick if I were you, old boy,' Victor chipped in, bent on substance-induced petty revenge for Summerscale's flirtation with the Swede. 'There are bigger Slav fish in our dear old Londongrad than him. Except, sod it, I am wrong. Not exactly Slav.' He turned towards the central table so pointedly that all of us, including Fynch and the Russian, followed his gaze. Just at that moment Natalia was saying something to Gorsky. Although they were seated at least a foot apart, their faces were lit with a desire that was impossible to mistake.

Summerscale's face turned deep crimson as he watched them. He stood up, pushed the chair away and walked noisily back to his table. Gorsky glanced at his bodyguards. The room went quiet.

'Sorry to interrupt your conversation, dear boy,' Summerscale hissed loudly enough to be heard at our end of the room, then paused. Gorsky waited. Natalia stared at the floral centrepiece. In a flash, Summerscale seemed to change his mind. Slumping into his chair, he laughed, and said, 'Never mind. Never mind.'

Before anyone had time to relax, he switched over to Russian – English accented, but still loud and clear, 'Keep your dirty Yid paws off my wife. Do you hear me?'

Natalia's expression, frozen as she awaited Gorsky's response, confirmed that I had understood the remark. I saw Gorsky look at her, then at Summerscale, then at the bodyguards, then back at her, weighing a decision. Summerscale's lips stretched into a forced smile. Gorsky still stared at Natalia. Some kind of wordless conversation was taking place between them.

'What did you just say to Uncle Roman, Daddy?' Daisy said in English. Natalia whispered something in her ear.

A team of waiters entered with dessert plates covered with silver cloches. The maître d'hôtel looked at Gorsky for a sign. Gorsky nodded.

'Yes,' he said. 'Yes. We are ready.'

As the guests started moving towards the ballroom for the auction, I used the moment to slip away. For once, it wasn't raining. In St James's Park, couples sat on picnic blankets and drank wine from plastic glasses. A lone violinist – a busker from somewhere in my part of the world – was playing a familiar czárdás. I stood for a long while, listening to the music. Stars glimmered faintly in a long-lost battle with city lights. The vast wheel of the London Eye revolved slowly above the treetops.

'When I was a child in Russia, they used to play music from public speakers. People danced in the streets. Just simple passers-by: they dropped their burden for a moment and followed the sound. Those times were not all bad. Far from it.'

I was startled to hear Gorsky beside me. He seemed not to be angry with me after all.

'Have all the donkeys gone?' I asked.

He looked at me as though I was raving.

'How was the auction?' I rephrased the question.

'Good, good . . .' he said. Clearly the auction was not what troubled him.

'I was thirteen, you know, when I first knew I was a Jew. Someone used that same word about me at school and I did not even respond . . . I thought they were talking about someone else. My parents were Communists and atheists. If you asked about religion, and very few people did ask in those days, that's what they said. Gorsky is not even a particularly Jewish name. I am hardly going to hide my Jewishness, don't misunderstand – quite the opposite is true – but I am Russian first. I am as devoted to Mother Russia, and I gave as much to it, as any Orthodox Slav, more than most of them, in fact.'

I knew little of Judaism and had no thoughts about degrees of Russianness. If they were all so devoted to Russia – her Christians and Jews alike – why were they spending their millions in London? Even hearing him say 'Mother Russia' in English and without irony sounded strange.

'I am sure Tom Summerscale is not anti-Semitic,' I said. 'Or, rather, not really. He does not mean it. He was just thrashing about. He has that peculiarly English prejudice towards anyone who is "not one of us", yet people like him hate other English people even more than us, because they don't judge us in the same way as they do their own. Whenever English people open their mouths they reveal the opening chapters of their autobiographies to each other, but we just brand ourselves as foreign. He wants to offend you, and how else could he possibly offend you? He can't call you a filthy Russian. He is married to one.'

I am not sure why I persisted in my defence of Summerscale, such as it was. Gorsky was clearly untroubled by him. It was as though I was trying to defend a mosquito that had bitten him.

'I have helped synagogues in this town, and I have attended a service or two, got to understand a bit more than the nothing I knew before. But I have endowed a handful of Orthodox monasteries, too, back in Russia and on Mount Athos. It's more about helping to preserve beauty than about God, I suppose. How can you be anything but agnostic? When I marry . . . I am not going to expect my wife, or my child, to convert to Judaism. If she should expect me to marry in church, even to be baptised myself, I would consider it—' A deep, tormented shiver sounded in his voice as he said this. He spoke as though he was rehearsing an argument.

'That seems most unlikely,' I interrupted. He was torturing himself.

He looked at me. He did not seem to understand what I meant. I found it difficult to mention Natalia's name.

'It is most unlikely that she would want to marry in a church. Particularly given her divorce . . .'

'What do you mean? It was just convenience, her arrangement with the Englishman. He is so unimportant that I can't even feel angry with him. We'll forget all of that.'

'It is sometimes impossible to forget. There are actions you can't undo. You can't set the clock back.'

'I see that you are not a scientist, Nikolai,' he laughed. 'Of course you can.'

8

Things went quiet after that evening. Weeks went by and nothing happened. Even Gery wasn't sure why. At first she told me that Natalia wanted to send Daisy away to a summer camp, some kind of etiquette school for little goddesses on Lake Geneva, and only then break the news to Summerscale. The beginning of the summer holidays, two months away, would make the announcement less disruptive for the child. Then Gery thought Natalia might have wavered in the face of the sheer strength of Gorsky's determination. It was as though she was trying to find a way to appease the Fates. In spite of Gorsky's reticence, there was something so elemental about his drive that it scared her. It belonged to another era, Gery quoted her, like the ransacking of Troy. This cannot end well, she kept repeating.

I am not sure why Gorsky waited, but wait he did. What are two months compared to ten years? During those two months, his building project was slowly completed. The intricacy of Xiulan Xi's design was beginning to reveal itself to the world. Open-top buses stopped and people stood up to take photographs. Planting and ornate ironwork would soon hide the vast residential wings from every angle other than that afforded by the windows of what was still – just about – my bedroom.

One day I saw the workmen deliver two huge baths carved out of rock crystal. Their shapes were complementary, like lovers' seats, as though they were meant to be installed side by side so that the bathers could face each other. Then there was a week when they kept bringing in chandeliers, with long pendulous diamond drops – dozens of chandeliers, then hundreds of matching wall lamps and candelabra. In due course the gardeners moved in, delivering huge mature trees, hiding away corners with pergolas and dotting alcoves with antique sculptures, while rolling out sections of rich green turf like expensive carpets.

My turn came, too. I abandoned my desk at Fynch's to start moving the books into the library – a vast hall, which, through a couple of hidden doorways, connected the private wings with the gallery space. I now had a stay of execution in the gatekeeper's cottage – rent free – until I had finished the task of shelving.

My commute to work became very short. I crossed the gravel path towards 'Château Gorsky' each morning. I unpacked boxes and placed the titles in the order I had been planning for many months. Some went on open shelves, others were displayed, with the help of consultants from the British Library, in sealed glass cabinets with controlled temperature and humidity. Some of the precious volumes were opened on a particular page in their display cases. They bore handwritten annotations or dedications with signatures so familiar that they looked fake. Tolstoy, Dostoevsky, Chekhov, Lermontov, Turgenev, Goethe, Donne, Byron, Balzac: I ensured that Gorsky's literary idols – and those who could be his idols – were all there. I included writers he enjoyed, like Dickens and Scott, neither of whom I cared for at all, but I also smuggled in slim volumes by my own heroes, often retiring small-time clerks, or booksellers like me, people like Kafka and Cavafy, Saba and Svevo, Pessoa and Walser. One day, he might even find the time to read them and remember me.

Framed in a little mahogany box, with an ornate lid inlaid with Siberian gemstones, was the manuscript that represented the collector's Koh-i-noor: Pushkin's poem of undying love for Anna Kern, the very sheet that the poet tucked between the pages of *Eugene Onegin* when he presented the book to Anna on the day of their parting. I overheard Gorsky recite the opening verse to Natalia when they met at Fynch's. It was, and even then by virtue of citation, the only time I heard him address her with an informal *you*.

I own up to pangs of pride as 'my' library took its final shape. I had a guilty secret. I inscribed my signature, in Serbian Cyrillic, on the title page of a first edition of Hazlitt's *Spirit of the Age*, the theme of my futile doctoral dissertation. It was a desecration, like Rimbaud's graffito on the pillar in Luxor, which I could not resist and which I would not have dared inflict on any of the Russian greats. In hindsight, I recognise that Gorsky had already started to change me. I was beginning to care. I wanted both of them to remember me.

I was in the Barracks early one morning, scrolling through one of the many lists of titles, when a removal van arrived. A couple of burly Russians carried in Gorsky's personal possessions: files, a baby grand piano, an old-fashioned record player, then clothes in zippered covers, shoes, boots, several hat-boxes . . . I stood and watched. Gorsky's personal 'stuff' amounted cumulatively to less than my own. Was he not that keen on ownership after all, or was he extremely good at getting rid of things? It took four or five trips to and from a modest white van. Compared to everything that had already been delivered to the house, this was positively ascetic.

Then the familiar majestic car arrived and the man himself stepped out with a bottle of champagne. I was soon summoned by a solitary butler to an enormous and – but for the piano already installed in the corner – completely empty room. Gorsky approached me with two glasses.

'You are my house-warming party,' he said.

'To the move!' I responded, taking a sip of a Grande Cuvée. By then, I had come to know the difference. 'I hope I will get a guided tour when it's furnished.'

'Oh, that will wait a little while longer. You need a woman's touch to furnish a woman's home.'

'To homeliness, then,' I said. One would need to be an interior decorator of genius to make these football pitches homely.

'I am keeping my place outside London for the moment.' I assumed that he was referring to that former Bishop's palace, which had six pages in Pevsner to itself. 'I have a few acres of forest down there and a natural swimming pool. It can be oppressive in town during the summer yet I don't want to leave Britain more often than I have to until everything is sorted out.' I wondered if anything could possibly dent his optimism.

I invited him to view his library. We started from the large alcove that housed the Romantics. He seemed to me to be one of them, in spite of the way in which he spoke of his 'narrow, mathematical mind'. I held up a copy of Goethe's *Faust* which used to belong to Shelley. I reeled off amusing anecdotes which involved the Brits, the French and the Germans, and I occasionally invoked the Russians as if to suggest that the best that Europe had ever produced was now in his possession.

I hope it won't sound immodest, but that impromptu talk was more impressive than my viva all those years ago. I was hoping that he would appreciate the story his collection – our collection – was telling, that he would acknowledge that, like Cyrano, I had created something that would, if our Roxane or anyone else bothered to look, go on seducing on his behalf. Yet he followed my explanations absentmindedly, exclaiming *well done, well done* intermittently, glancing across the road towards The Laurels more often than at the shelves. He perked up only when I mentioned Natalia, but he realised that I was speaking of Puskhin as he lay dying after the duel with the French baron who had tried to cuckold him.

'Ah, you mean Natalia Pushkina,' he said almost dismissively, as though Pushkin's wife had little claim to her own Christian name.

He lifted a slim volume with an inlaid medallion, briefly examined a faded lock of two-centuries-old hair, and dropped the book on the window sill. It was as though he had lost interest in the project. Even when I opened that precious edition of *Onegin*, the one he had been so keen on acquiring, he barely looked at it.

Gorsky started disappearing for days at a time. He was in the country or away on business: Moscow, Zurich, Berlin, Jerusalem, Almaty. In between the jaunts he popped in, delivering a gift of an expensive bottle that could have come from anywhere as though he was trying to placate me in some way, or pretending to check on me, but was unfazed if he found me with my nose buried in a collection of Russian poetry or a Victorian travel book. I was not expected back at Fynch's just yet, and he did not seem to mind my increasingly obvious freeloading.

'*Ivanushka, durachok,*' he laughed when I asked why he tolerated me – *little Ivan, little ninny* – as though I was a useless younger brother and not an employee.

On the mornings after some of those nights he spent in residence, I could smell a woman's scent on the corridors, a faint, powdery smell of mimosas, Natalia's smell. I found a pair of sunglasses on one of the shelves. In the evenings, I looked out but saw only lights going on or off. I heard music, old Russian waltzes, simple tunes. I suspected that Gorsky played them himself.

Once, I crept up almost to the open window. I stood on the grass barefoot and recognised the chords of 'Dark is the Night', a melancholy Russian love song from the Second World War. I thought I heard a female voice as well. I tried to climb on one of the marble pots to look in, when a bodyguard gripped me and pulled me back a few yards by the scruff of my neck.

'You think we don't see you, *malchik* . . . We do, but we let you hear the boss play the tune because we understand. We love to hear him play too. Now run away before he finds you here.'

The second May bank holiday brought an unseasonal, and short-lived, hot spell. The air was heady with the sweet scent of lime trees, which that year, in spite of the endless rain, came to flower earlier and more profusely than I had ever remembered in London before. One Saturday morning Tom Summerscale unexpectedly decided to make his peace. Gery claimed that he felt chastened. Rumours about his overwrought behaviour and his insult of Gorsky were not going down well in his business circles. It was not the done thing. He had too much capital invested in Russia not to care. He sent a note of apology to Gorsky.

Then, in a further gesture of contrition, he instructed Gery to invite Gorsky and me to his rooftop swimming pool. Gorsky, even more unexpectedly, accepted. The pool was small and secluded within the walls of a former hospital chapel on the top floor, giving the lie to the wondering gossip about the slide to the basement pool.

It had an ingenious retractable glass roof and beyond the walls it was surrounded by a roof garden modelled on the Alhambra. In the course of my year among the Russians, I had become accustomed to architectural flights of fancy, but this was a revelation. To swim with a view of Gothic-revival mosaics of Christian saints, no doubt the source of those jumbled stories I heard months ago, and sunbathe surrounded by jasmine, while in the middle of London: how can the human capacity for happiness continue to take in such luxuries?

Only Daisy and I swam. Natalia reclined under a white parasol. She was leafing through some glossy magazine too thick to be held up, so she rested it on a boyish hip and faced away from the rest of us. She must have been aware of the strangeness of the situation, and her body – exposed though it was to our collective gaze – responded by pretending it wasn't there. She was wearing a dark blue swimsuit whose plain cut was more suited to water polo than to the pool on a Chelsea rooftop. The movement of her right shoulder blade as she turned the pages was the only sign that she was alive.

Gery sunbathed in a tiny crimson bikini consisting of minute triangles connected by straps thinner than shoelaces, as she must have done many times already. The tan of her bronze-aged body was the colour of milky coffee. Gorsky and Summerscale sat side by side in huge garden armchairs. They sipped their whiskies in silence; Summerscale in striped swimming trunks, with white trails of sun cream on his wide shoulders, Gorsky in jeans and a linen shirt. An awkward straw hat hid the upper half of his face. He was sunning only his bare feet.

Then Daisy invited us all to play a board game. Her mother declined and disappeared inside, promising that she would be back in a minute, but did not return. Gery followed her in a bit later. Gorsky, Summerscale and I indulged the girl. It was a sort of Snakes and Ladders involving miniature plastic rabbits and a huge red dice. We tried surreptitiously to ensure that she won every time. She yelped, counting alternately in Russian and English as she moved the figures on our behalf. We slowly relaxed into the simple rhythm of the game.

Summerscale and Gorsky found themselves

imprisoned in the same square for three rounds while Daisy and I raced ahead. It was the first time since the auction that I saw the two men engage in something you could describe as the beginnings of a conversation. Then Daisy cast the dice and it rolled off the table together with the board pieces. She reached below to collect the figures and squealed: 'Look, everyone, look!'

She moved the table away. The three of us followed the direction of her index finger.

'Look. Uncle Roman's feet!'

Gorsky's feet were long and narrow, and at first glance there was nothing remarkable about them. He had a high instep and his toes were almost as long as Daisy's fingers. But his small toe was disproportionately tiny and turned inwards in a way that made it look as though it was made of plasticine and attached as an afterthought to the foot itself.

'The girl has found your Achilles heel, Roman. So to speak.' I had never quite managed to call him by his first name before.

To amuse her, he wiggled his toes as though he was

playing an imaginary piano with them. Summerscale's face darkened. He stood up and walked away. Daisy took the seat he had vacated and, sitting side by side with Gorsky, started imitating him. The sight of her feet stopped me in my tracks. Gorsky tickled the girl's right foot with his left, one silly plasticine toe next to another, much smaller but otherwise identical, one.

'You are a clever little girl, you know, Margaritka,' he said in Russian, using the Russian word for daisy. 'My clever little girl.'

I did the maths quickly amid the stunned silence. The suggestion, which I did not dare articulate even to myself, was utterly impossible. *Poor, deluded soul*, I thought. In the months and weeks that followed, I never forgot his tone.

He and I sat with the girl for quite a while, abandoned by our hosts. She had fallen asleep in her chair, and Gorsky covered her with a beach towel. Below us, the streets of London hummed with activity. Voices and sirens and the screeching of tyres melded in a distant symphony. Then

Summerscale re-emerged, his mood completely changed. He was fully dressed and almost euphoric as he walked towards Gorsky and patted him forcefully on the back.

'I am sorry I left you, old boy. I remembered something that needed to be resolved instantly. But it's all sorted. We need to get moving. I told Natalia to get ready. We can't sit here on a day like this. London belongs to us.' He uttered that last sentence in Russian and raised his arm towards the surrounding roofs, which seemed to pulsate with human energy. He lifted Daisy in her towel, and she hugged him without waking up, lowering her head on his rugby player's shoulder. Gorsky said nothing.

'Nick and I will go ahead,' Summerscale said, 'and grab a table at the Cabana in Notting Hill. Would you like to bring Natalia when she is ready? Gery will look after Daisy.'

The promise of being alone in the car with Natalia must have tipped the scales. Gorsky nodded. I could hardly demur. I pulled my jeans and T-shirt on and laced up my plimsolls, then Summerscale and I walked down several flights of servants' stairs to the underground garage. It housed the familiar silver limo, the Land Rover in which Summerscale had driven me back from Notting Hill once before, a two-seater sports car of some make I did not recognise, a motorcycle, a couple of Vespas and a blue hatchback. The little car was dusty and full of clutter. I had assumed it was driven by one of their servants. Summerscale surprised me by jumping into it.

'Gery and I use this baby whenever we are up to no good,' Summerscale explained. 'I don't mean together, my dear man. Although I wouldn't say that we haven't tried. It seems that we don't find each other exciting enough. All that muscle, urgh.'

He was a changed man all right. He had reverted to his usual vile self.

The automated gate opened and we merged with the London traffic. No one gave us a second glance as we drove through South Kensington and across the park towards the warren behind Ladbroke Grove. I assumed we were going straight to the Cabana, but Summerscale paused in front of a familiar house.

'I am sure you will remember my accountant?' He winked. 'Do come along to say hello. Safety in numbers!'

Allaoui opened the front door himself. He was in the same bournous and wore the same pair of trainers on his sockless feet as last time. He said nothing and gave no indication of recognising me. He was in a bad mood, but he invited us in and seated us in a surprisingly neat little kitchen. We declined an offer of mint tea. When he disappeared into the back of the house, Summerscale lit a cigarette and I stared at a calendar with the picture of some unfamiliar walled town by the sea. There was a caption in Arabic and French partly obscured by a large blue glass pendant, an amulet to ward off the evil eye. Next to it hung several framed photographs of two apparently English kids, a boy and a girl of about ten or twelve, in blue school shirts and stripy neckties, casting forced smiles towards the camera. Their pale chubby faces and lanky hair made it evident that they had no connection with our host. I looked at Summerscale. He shrugged. He appeared to have no idea who they were and, even more clearly, did not care. The house was silent. We could hear the shuffling of Allaoui's trainers as he returned to the kitchen. He followed my eyes to the calendar.

'Essaouira, Morocco, the most beautiful town in the world,' Allaoui said, as though my interest in the picture had pierced the cloud of his foul mood. It was the first time he had registered my presence.

'Where you from?' he asked, and gave no indication of recognition when I mentioned my birthplace. Nonetheless, he must have realised that I was not English because something akin to warmth flickered in his eyes.

'You know how hard it is for us then. How hard to live here. Everyone thinks we are just monkeys come down from banana trees. Es Sauira, yes.' He now said it as two words and sighed. 'This town is nothing, and you and I are nothing in it, my friend.'

He pushed another envelope across the table towards Summerscale.

'The best you are likely to get in this town, Mr Sumicale,' he said.

'Let's give you the Swiss then.' Summerscale counted

several five-hundred-franc notes, then left them on one of the little doilies that dotted the surface of the table.

'Where's the missis?' he asked, casually, as he stuffed the envelope in his pocket.

Allaoui squealed like a wounded animal, hit his chest with a fist a couple of times, then started cursing as though Summerscale had just punched him in the solar plexus.

'That fucking whore,' he shouted, somehow gaining greater English fluency in his rage. 'I locked that prostitute inside her bedroom a week ago. I will let her out when she admits that she has been cheating. She swears she is faithful, but she is an English whore. She is lucky I haven't killed her yet. All English women are whores. I'd never have married the bitch but for her fucking passport.'

He composed himself as quickly as he had lost his temper. He gave an ingratiating smile.

'I am sorry, Mr Sumicale. I am touched by your care.'

He escorted us out. Although I had some sympathy with Allaoui in view of what I knew of his wife's activities, I was sufficiently concerned for her safety to wonder aloud if we should call the police. Summerscale laughed it off.

'Oh, I have seen worse from Mahdi, old boy. Much worse. They love each other in their crazy way, as much as I love my own missis. You know what Tolstoy wrote about happy families? He was wrong. The unhappy ones are all the same. We must allow the happy ones to be happy in their own ways.'

To this day I regret that I did nothing, but the subsequent drama of that evening wiped out Janice Allaoui's predicament. When we arrived, the Notting Hill bar was heaving with a smart cosmopolitan crowd. Waiters in guayaberas held trays of cocktails high above their heads: glasses of brightly coloured liquid decorated with paper parasols, sparklers and pieces of tropical fruit. The place was postmodern and 'ironical' in that greedy, calculating way which was never a sufficient excuse to charge fifteen pounds for a glass of something nasty, however skilfully it had been PR-ed as 'the place to be'. Only the music was genuine, and, luckily, not particularly loud. Summerscale ordered for both of us, and we sat together in silence sipping something green with a lot of tequila until Natalia and Gorsky arrived.

They were both in jeans and white shirts. She wore a pair of red trainers of some fashionable make. Her hair was gathered on top of her head with a white ribbon tied in the kind of knot Russian schoolgirls used to wear back in Communist days. She walked slowly, without making the smallest effort to look happy. Gorsky, on the other hand, practically glowed. I was struck, although God knows it was for the umpteenth time, by how tall she was. They were almost of equal height, even though Gorsky was certainly six foot if not an inch or two taller. I noticed, and Summerscale probably did too, that Gorsky's hand rested on her back as they made their way through the crowd. That gesture may have been the reason why, almost as soon as they were seated, he started talking about the beauty of Russian women. They were the most beautiful in the world, the best educated, passionate, innately elegant . . . as he counted superlatives, Natalia looked more and more uncomfortable.

'The best tractor drivers and cosmonauts too.' I made a feeble effort to bring in the Communist stereotype and redirect the flow of his speech. Natalia threw me a half-smile.

'But most importantly,' Summerscale ploughed on, 'they are not poisoned by feminism. They are real women and proper, obedient wives to their husbands. Pity about the Russian men . . .'

'Why?' enquired Gorsky.

'Neanderthal oafs,' Summerscale said, as though he wasn't speaking to a Russian. 'No wonder Russian women prefer Western men. They would rather marry an ordinary Englishman than a Russian millionaire. Wouldn't they, Nick?'

I could only point out that someone like me must be at the bottom of the food chain however you calibrated it.

Gorsky had had enough.

'This Russian woman prefers a Russian man to you, Summerscale.'

At least he did not say *me*. Natalia stood up to leave but he put his hand on her right shoulder and she froze in her seat. Her left hand hovered over his as though she was unsure whether to remove it or to grasp it. The wedding band, which she usually wore on her left hand – rather than the right, the Russian way – was no longer on her ring finger.

'Russian man, you say . . .' Summerscale laughed. 'Oh, well, even if we accept that you are Russian, Roman, and that's a questionable proposition, why did she marry me then? She is a refined soul, our Natalie, and you know it. She doesn't want a Yid arms smuggler, all that blood on her hands.'

Gorsky's fist put a stop to Summerscale's speech. The blow was so forceful that Summerscale's body, together with the chair he was sitting on, flew into the air before landing on the floor with a massive thud. The crowd fell silent. Gorsky's bodyguards, whose presence was so constant I had long stopped registering them, stepped menacingly closer. The strength of Gorsky's blow was such that they may well have wondered why he needed them. Natalia ran out even before one of the waiters ordered the three of us to leave and threatened to call the police if we didn't. I straightened the chairs. Gorsky pulled a wad of fifty-pound notes from his pocket and left them on the table, crumpled, red fingerprints all over the red paper. The waiter turned towards Summerscale who was just standing up, clearly hoping that he wouldn't have to call the police after all. Summerscale blew his bloody nose into a paper napkin, dropped it over the money, then grabbed my arm and walked out. On our left, already almost at the top of Portobello Road, I could see Gorsky catching up with Natalia, remonstrating.

Summerscale drove in the opposite direction. We were soon stuck in lanes of traffic on Shepherd's Bush roundabout. I watched people in red buses, slumped and drowsy in the unexpected heat of the evening. It was nice to be in an ordinary car, for once free from that insistent gaze with which the poor follow the movement of the rich in their midst, but that was the only pleasant aspect of my situation. We were cramped too close to each other. Summerscale tapped restlessly on the steering wheel. I could see a streak of dried blood below the signet ring on his little finger. There was another thinner line on his cheek, stretching from his nose towards his ear.

'You seem fond of that word,' I said. I did not know how to start talking about the situation. There was an air of bonhomie about him which I took for an ironic upper-class take on being a spiv. It misled you into thinking that he was more approachable than Gorsky, yet this was far from true. I felt uncomfortable about the things he had allowed me to witness. Did he think that he was invulnerable or that he had me in his power in some way? That he could trump the knowledge of him I had involuntarily acquired? Or was he, simply, stupid? You needed to be the king of crooks to carry on semi-publicly with your drug dealer's wife and to keep visiting him at home, bringing your so-called friends along. To be the king of crooks, monumentally stupid, or to feel protected in some way I could not begin to fathom. Or perhaps just to be English.

'What?' he asked impatiently. 'What word?'

I could see that he knew, but I repeated it anyway.

'Yid. You are very fond of the word Yid. What are you hoping to achieve with it? Change Natalia's mind?'

He snorted as he changed gears.

'I am sorry about that, Nick, old chap. I am not proud of myself, but I feel safe. I know what I was saying. There is no way she would leave me for that man, billions or not. He will forever remind her of borscht and poverty, and he knows it too. Why do you think she called our daughter Daisy? She doesn't even like to speak Russian if she can help it.'

We moved on. A group of young boys emerged from an underpass. Only God and they themselves knew what they were up to at this hour. The railings separating us from them were decorated with metal cut-outs of sheep. The animals were supposed to look jolly, like something in a playground, yet the effect was depressing. You could not but see them for what they were: a dismal effort to evoke the memory of the pastures which had lent the ugly concrete junction their name.

Five days later, Janice Allaoui disappeared.

I picked up the free newspaper from a stand at Sloane Square station. At first, I did not even notice the item, buried deep on page sixteen. The following morning, leafing through yesterday's news in search of a book review I had flagged up, I spotted the familiar smiling face, the picture cut out of a wedding photograph.

West London woman reported missing: it was the sort of

article one ignores every day, and only reads if it concerns someone in one's own neighbourhood, sometimes not even then. The groom's shoulder was truncated but an arm was still visible around hers, a male hand just above her elbow. Judging by the skin colour, it wasn't Allaoui's. And Janice Allaoui wasn't wearing a bridal gown but a white jacket. You knew that the occasion was a wedding from the posy of silk flowers tucked into a pile of locks carefully arranged above her ear. The ornament was simple enough to make one uncertain whether she was the bride or an ageing bridesmaid – still lively, still attractive – if plump blondes were your sort of thing, an English tulip rather than an English rose.

The picture must have been taken some years ago, but Janice was already in her mid thirties. Slightly flushed or slightly drunk, clearly happy, she looked into the camera with the feistiness and insouciance I remembered from that strange evening in Soho with Summerscale. Her loop earrings reflected the light of the flash so that there was around her neck a sort of halo which merged with the smoke from a cigarette she was holding some inches away from her mouth. Her other hand, arm and most of her left shoulder had been cropped in an editorial bid to get rid of any traces of her companion.

I phoned Gery immediately. We had just met in a pub when, on a TV screen above the bar, Allaoui appeared in a press conference, looking every inch the wife-beater and murderer. He had probably strangled her and dumped her body into Regent's Canal, or buried it in an unmarked grave in Kensal Green. He had made no secret of his intentions when I last saw him – he had said that she was lucky he hadn't got rid of her. His involvement in the murder was so obvious that the police must have interviewed him the moment his wife was reported missing. Why were they letting him parade this pretence of grief?

The sound was off, but Gery's eyes were glued to the screen. Allaoui was flanked by a policeman on one side and two official-looking types on the other: detectives, or lawyers, I couldn't tell. The Met must have played its cards carefully to avoid hurting racial sensitivities. The policeman was an Arab, as handsome as Adonis in his dark blue uniform. The English guys looked like a couple of spuds next to him.

Allaoui was a good five inches shorter than the shortest of them, and he wore a ridiculous electric-blue suit of some shiny material, unmatched by a green shirt with a big round collar, and a pink polka-dot tie with a wide knot, which looked as though it was about to choke him. He was unshaven, uncombed, red eyed and bewildered.

'This town is nothing, and you and I are nothing in it, my friend,' I could almost hear him again. The ticker at the bottom of the screen repeated the basic details of the case. Camera lights flashed. One of the men held a sheet of paper and read from it, then Allaoui descended from a kind of lectern-podium, looking even smaller, like a cross between a ten-year-old boy and a pub bouncer. The camera zoomed in on his face and he gazed steadily into it. I felt as though he had intuited that this was a staring contest between him and me. His eyes welled with tears, while he watched, fixedly, for a couple of beats, then crumpled, like a balloon deflating, into the arms of a policeman who guided him away from the crowd and the cameras.

'What an act!' I said.

'You know this man, Nick,' Gery said. 'Do you? He looks like a drug dealer. Do you know him?'

I couldn't quite work out if she really had no idea.

'Yes. I mean no. Someone I know knows him,' I stammered. 'All I know is that I don't expect his wife is alive.'

Gery stared at me for a moment, then for some unaccountable reason decided not to press on.

'It's a cruel city. People do all sorts to survive. They deal, they steal. If they are men. If they are women, they sell their bodies. One way or another, we all end up doing it. We make unsuitable choices, or the sale goes wrong. I expect you are right about her death. They are tough, women like that one, they don't just run away from home.'

9

The next day the ghastly plot took another turn. I was in a department store in Sloane Square. I raised my eyes from my purchase and saw – multiplied on several rows of TV screens of different kinds and sizes – the familiar face of Janice's sister, red with hysteria and tears. The camera zoomed out to take in her interviewer, a Chinese girl in a pair of vertiginous heels, and I realised that they were standing in the doorway of a block of flats in Covent Garden. I had to get home. I dropped everything and ran down four flights of escalators and along the King's Road. I was out of breath when I switched on my little TV and collapsed into the chair in front of it. I had a good idea what I was about to hear.

In a repeat of the interview that was going to play on the hour every hour for the rest of the day, Sal was describing the way she had discovered her sister's body. She had been reluctant to go to the flat, although she had the keys. She feared that she was being watched. She kept calling her sister's mobile. She was convinced that Janice was on the run, because of her husband's threats. She waited for her sister to return her calls. Then, as the days went by, she could wait no longer.

The moment she opened the door of the flat, she knew. Her sister's body was on the sofa, face down. The room was a mess of upended furniture and breakages. Janice's nose was broken, and her face was bloody. She had clearly put up a fight. And she was wearing her favourite red Roland Mouret dress, Sal repeated on the loop, every hour, as though the designer's name held a vital clue.

Mahmoud Allaoui was still distressed but there was malicious glee in his misery when the focus of the inquiry moved to Tom Summerscale. He couldn't have suspected that his wife was having an affair with an English gentleman of Summerscale's calibre, he said, but he clearly wasn't astounded either.

'I am devastated,' he added, in his heavily accented English, 'to lose my beloved wife in this way. Devastated that she was found in the flat of Mr Summerscale with whom I have had business dealings over a number of years. But if she was unfaithful to me, then I am not at all sorry to see her dead. There is only one punishment for adultery.'

That last sentence – part accusation, part confession – was replayed many times over the photographs of Janice and Summerscale now set side by side, yet looking like the most unlikely adulterous couple imaginable. They were occasionally juxtaposed with a picture of Natalia and Daisy. Although the child's face was pixelated, the image seemed like a still from some glamorous Hollywood film, an illustration for the next news item, a mistake.

I declined the call handler's offer of an interpreter

when I dialled the Freephone number provided in the police appeal which followed Allaoui's press conference. I volunteered to go to the station and I gave my statement to a couple of officers who were an image – a caricature almost – of British decency. A solicitous young policewoman noted my words down. Her handwriting was as round as her waistline. Her body was bursting out of her uniform as keenly as her ginger curls kept escaping the bun at the back of her head. Her male colleague nodded when I tried to explain why I felt that Allaoui was a liar, although I had no evidence for it. *I see what you mean, Mr Kimović*, he repeated a couple of times, only to follow up with questions which suggested that he didn't. The cameras buzzed on, but I had become so used to CCTV in those months with Gorsky that I was barely noticing them.

They offered telephone numbers and leaflets explaining what to do if I was summoned to provide a longer statement, or if I was called to court. If I felt I needed someone to talk to, they said, they had trained counsellors offering their services in a range of languages. The only psychological advice I am likely to need, I mused sourly, was how to live with a feeling that I might have just made Natalia's life harder than it was already.

Details about Tom Summerscale dribbled out. His career as a legal advisor to powerful Russian business interests, his glamorous lifestyle, his young Russian wife, even his first wife and her undeniably decent Englishness: at first everything seemed to indicate that he couldn't possibly have had anything to do with a murder as sordid as this. And Summerscale himself denied it adamantly. Yes, he knew her. Yes, they had even had sex on one or two occasions. It was pointless to deny that now, although a gentleman should never tell. Yes, she had the keys to his Covent Garden flat. Of course she did: she was looking after it. A caretaker. A cleaner, if you will. It did not need much cleaning because it was uninhabited. No, it wasn't unusual to own a house in Chelsea and a flat in Covent Garden. He had meant to let it out but had forgotten to do so. That wasn't unusual either. London property was a good investment, it did not need to be put to work. No, he hadn't been there in weeks. And no, he had no idea how often Mrs Allaoui went there alone or how much she was paid for her caretaking duties. One of his managers took care of that.

I remained convinced of Summerscale's innocence even after the victim's sister gave another interview, adding to her original story and implicating him further, allowing the media reports to continue titillating their audiences while stopping short of any formal accusation. It is a lie that Janice was just some servant, just a cleaner, Sal said. You don't take cleaners to expensive restaurants and present them with designer clothes: at that she waved a picture of Janice in a pink Chanel suit she claimed was a gift from Summerscale. She also asserted that he used to buy birthday presents for the spotty boy and girl whose photographs I had noticed on the wall of Janice's kitchen, the children of her first marriage. He might have had other lovers but Janice was, for many years, and long before he married the Russian and she married Allaoui, very special, almost, you could say, the perfect wife he had never had. She certainly took better care of him, Sal ploughed on, than the Russian, who couldn't look after a guinea pig if you asked her to.

Three or four 'friends', all flunkeys like me, came out of the woodwork to confirm the truthfulness of Sal's story. Like me, they were all at some point or other entertained by Summerscale, part of the same strange 'happy household' routine he seemed to have indulged Janice with. It was both deeper and stranger than the usual tales of extramarital sex. He enjoyed being mothered and pampered by her, and he was generous in return, taking her out, sometimes with her sister, to the kind of smart places where a woman like her stood out more than a glossy model. He was also, it seemed undeniable, sexually attracted to her, in spite of – or perhaps because of – her cheerful commonness. Why would he keep her as his mistress otherwise?

Sal's claims provoked more public animosity directed at Summerscale's life of thoughtless privilege than there ever was for Allaoui's pleas of an immigrant's hard luck, which he used to justify every unsavoury move he made. Who else could have killed the poor deluded woman, suddenly everyone seemed to ask, but Thomas Summerscale? There was no sign of forced entry to the flat and he was the only person who both had the keys to it and knew that Janice would be there. His DNA was all over the place. An obvious motive was still lacking, but he was the obvious culprit.

The most unexpected response to such allegations came from Summerscale's first wife. While Natalia remained, for public purposes, unavailable and aloof, her photographs flashing intermittently like sightings of Yeti footprints, her predecessor agreed to be interviewed in front of her Gloucestershire cottage, under trailing wisteria, the image of a gracefully ageing Home Counties belle in a green waxed jacket, stroking a chocolate Labrador as she spoke. She asserted that Tom Summerscale was a 24-carat cad but no, not a murderer, definitely not a murderer. No, not even in the heat of passion. Never.

In spite of her valiant effort, he was taken into custody.

The completion of my Gorsky assignment could not be deferred for much longer. I still walked dutifully to work from my now rent-free accommodation every morning but, once inside the Barracks, I spent most of my time by the library windows, looking over towards The Laurels, hoping to catch sight of Natalia or Gery. Although I knew they were there, the house looked completely deserted. Even the paparazzi now lingered aimlessly by their stepladders, smoking and dropping empty crisp packets on the pavement.

It was during one such moment that Gorsky walked in on me. He seemed startled to see me. He looked as though he hadn't slept in days. His entire body exuded tension. His hands were tucked into his coat pockets at an unnatural angle. His white shirt was unbuttoned and his clavicles seemed raised, with deep dark pools behind them. They made the base of his neck look bruised, as if someone had been attempting to strangle him too. He apologised for disturbing me, absurdly, for I was clearly not working while supposedly still in his pay. I stammered something apologetic in turn.

'No matter, no matter . . .' he interrupted me and stepped nearer to the French window.

'She . . .' he started.

I waited. I hadn't spoken to him since the body was

found. 'She' was likely to be Natalia. I knew from Gery that he had been on the phone to her practically all the time, begging to take her away from London. Antibes, Yalta, Eilat, Samarkand: she only needed to name the place. Instead, she just sobbed.

Late at night, I had seen him leave the Barracks on a motorcycle and disappear into the empty streets. Once, after Summerscale was arrested, I stayed by my window long enough to witness the motorcycle return an hour later. Gorsky parked across the road, made a phone call and the gate opened. It was an inconspicuous sight, a helmeted man on a motorcycle in unremarkable bikers' leathers – but for the oddness of the hour you would assume it was a courier coming to deliver something. Yet the sight of him alone out on the street was almost shocking. He must have dispensed with his bodyguards on his excursions for Natalia's sake. She did not conceal that she disliked the Russians in his entourage because they witnessed and understood more than she wanted anyone but him to know. That he would make himself vulnerable like that seemed to me a more solid testimony of what she meant to him than even the edifice we were standing in.

'She . . .' He continued after a long pause: 'She tells me that she knows that he had been unfaithful. That she had known all along. That it did not matter to her. That she knows he isn't the killer. That he couldn't have been. That he was with her every night and every day since that day at the pool. That he clung to her because he sensed that he was losing her. She had told the police already, but an alibi provided by his wife is not enough, it seems. They will – she believes – soon find something to nail Allaoui. And I am trying to help with that. But she is not helping me to help her. We must wait until this is over, she says. I must wait. So she says . . .'

He flinched when he uttered the word 'wife' and he swung the French doors as though he was going to shatter the glass, but then, at the last moment, caught them, gently brought them back together and walked out of the room.

The following day was to be my penultimate working day at the Barracks. In truth, calling it work had become even more of a misnomer than that military name was for Gorsky's sumptuous Schloss. After the sun went down, the maid brought in a tray of sandwiches and a silver teapot, part of a continuous array of treats Gorsky had arranged to make my so-called toil more bearable. I was aimlessly pacing up and down the vast room when he returned, looking even more tortured than he had on the previous day. He continued his speech almost exactly where he had left it.

'You may think me an idiot, Nikolai, a holy fool. I remember her at nineteen, the prettiest, cleverest girl you could imagine, all the more beautiful for remaining so noble in those hideous surroundings. Only in Russia – and God knows why – do you find such women. I was already beginning to mean something in business. The Yeltsin times were difficult, chaotic. It was easy to make money under Boris Nikolaevich – irresponsible drunken oaf that people now say he was – but just as easy to lose it, and more. Human life was cheaper than a gallon of oil. Natalia's father saved my life a couple of times. I owed him loyalty. And she was meant for me: this was a simple mathematical equation, something stronger than us. I owned a small flat in St Petersburg, a second-hand Mercedes, even some decent clothes – too ostentatious, perhaps. We all were in those days. What was the point of being rich otherwise? we thought. I was a child myself, I had no concept of modesty. I went around in an astrakhan coat which I received as a present from someone in the Kremlin who got it from the president of Azerbaijan, can you imagine? I went into diplomatic stores – they still had them – using a stolen Israeli passport, just to be able to purchase silk ties and Italian shoes. Would you believe it? Volkov asked me to look after her, and I promised I would. I am not sure I ever kept that promise.'

One of his bodyguards knocked at the door. Gorsky dismissed them for the night. Then he dismissed me.

'You did well with this library, Nikolai. I knew you would. I have learned to trust my instincts when I choose my people. I recognised that passion in you. Now go home and take some rest. You deserve it,' he said, though no one deserved rest less than me.

That was the last time I saw him alive.

I remember the last thing I said. 'You will get your girl, sir. Very soon. I hope the girl is worth it.'

I briefly looked around, almost as though I sensed that I would never see the library again. We could have been standing in the middle of the Palace at Versailles. I called him sir, half-seriously, half-mocking our strange arrangement. Somewhere along the way I had lost the last atom of any envy I had ever felt for him. He was far too bright to be this wealthy, and far too wealthy to be happy.

'Worth the wait, you mean?' he countered. 'For all this is as nothing compared to the wait.'

Then, as I was leaving, so quietly that I wasn't even sure he said it.

'The girl is already mine.'

It feels strange to say that the most important event in my life was one I witnessed only as a grainy image on CCTV. Although I had spent more time with Gorsky in that last year than perhaps anyone else on this planet, I knew little about him. His life remains a mystery. His death is a different matter. His last four or five minutes on this earth were caught on a film I played and replayed twenty, thirty, forty times a day, until I could no longer watch, until I knew the sequence so well that I did not need to watch it in order to see it. At first I tried to remember every detail, then I could not forget.

The scene shows nothing for a minute or so. The camera is somewhere high up, pointing downwards towards the paving stones. There is a path by the Chelsea Embankment, an iron railing behind which you see water, flowing murkily, throwing an occasional silvery spark. There are street lamps, old, black, clearly once gas-powered, their light so weak it barely registers. The film is greyish blue, like a sequence of X-rays. It comes from an American millionaire's security camera positioned on a wall that runs close to the river path. Two trees partly obscure the path in the corners of the frame. For some reason they look like birch trees to me, although they are probably not: there are few birches in London. The trunks are pale, criss-crossed with short black scars, like stigmata. The leaves are fleshy and serrated. Although the film is silent I can hear them clinking in the wind like coins. A man appears from under the crown of leaves on the left-hand side, walks along the path, leans over the railing, looks into the water for a couple of minutes. Then he turns and faces the camera, searches for something in his pocket, takes out a mobile phone, presses a button as if to call, but pauses, leans with his back against the railing, seemingly reading a message on its small screen. The faint glow lights the familiar Prussian profile. His blond hair looks almost white in its light. Dark circles around his eyes give his face a skull-like appearance. I am not sure if I imagine this, but it looks as though his lips are about to spread into a smile. He puts the phone back in his pocket, buttons up his jacket, and turns as if to continue walking along the path. At that moment a hooded figure runs towards him. He turns. The first flash of a blade catches his left shoulder, the second, the third, the fourth and the fifth sink under the ribs. The attacker grabs him, takes something out of his pocket, walks away slowly, throws the knife into the river. He is wearing a black balaclava, a black leather jacket, a pair of dark trousers on bow legs, and incongruously light trainers with dark stripes. The victim clutches his stomach. For a moment it looks as though he might fall over the railings and into the water, but he bends forward and drops on to the pavement, where he rests on his side, still clutching his stomach. His body curls up into a question mark. A dark circle, like molten tar, slowly spreads around him. The scene is empty for another couple of minutes. The body doesn't move. The Thames sparkles through the railings behind it and the leaves flutter as if to prove that time passes, that you cannot set the clock back.

Unlike Janice Allaoui, Roman Gorsky and his death captured the front pages immediately. And the inside pages. Pages of text and photographs, day after day. There were pictures of his houses and cars, of his Greek island, of his plane and his enormous yacht. There were attempts to calculate his wealth and explain the source of his money. There were photos of seemingly every party he had ever thrown. On several of them I recognised my own back or caught a glimpse of my profile in the crowd. There were photos of a much younger Gorsky standing next to a tank in front of the White House in

Moscow during the Yeltsin coup, wearing a ridiculous astrakhan coat, then an even older picture, in a clumsy suit and a clumsier tie, and with a pair of heavy dark-rimmed glasses, in front of a blackboard covered with mathematical equations.

Apparently there had been murder attempts before, in Tallinn and Tel Aviv. Why wasn't he wearing a bullet-proof vest that night? His bodyguards were not with him: did they know? What exactly did they know? Had he become careless? It was the Russian mafia, said a famous columnist, and listed a number of Gorsky's so-called friends, including the three I met at Hesperos playing cards, as potential paymasters. It was the FSB, said a Russophobe correspondent. The government liked to have the monopoly on arms deals, and Gorsky was no longer playing the game. It was neither, argued an old Soviet historian. Why would the FSB send an amateur with a knife to the Thames embankment on the off-chance that the oligarch might step out for a late walk alone? It was an attempted robbery gone wrong, said a guest in a breakfast talk show. God knows there were too many in London these days. What a paradox, when you think how these people come to London for safety. It was unlikely to be a robbery, someone now retired from Scotland Yard pointed out. You threaten and intimidate. You don't inflict multiple stab wounds in order to steal someone's mobile phone. London's Mayor reminded people that it was one of the safest capitals in the developed world. The police service was doing all it could to eradicate knife-crime.

At first no one made a connection with the Summerscale case, although the police promptly made a connection with me. Other than the killer himself, I was possibly the last person to see Gorsky alive. This time, my testimony involved hours of videotape, and officers who were going places much higher than the duo investigating Janice Allaoui's death. I told them about the bookshop, about the library commission, even about my holiday in Greece. I told them everything I knew about Tom and Natalia Summerscale, too, including the details of Gorsky's pursuit of Natalia, which had previously seemed beside the point. I could not withhold any part of the jigsaw as irrelevant any more, although I was well aware that what I had to say did not help Summerscale who was fighting his case against worsening odds.

It was Natalia, in fact, who inadvertently sealed her husband's fate, even as she fought to save him. Coming into the court house, she looked like a murder victim herself: shocked and pale beyond grief, beyond devastation. The policeman walking behind her kept raising his arms as if to catch her if she fainted on the stairs. In the courtroom, Allaoui became visibly agitated when Natalia confirmed that she wasn't troubled by her husband's dalliance with Janice Allaoui, and even more so when she added that no, she did not believe for a moment that Tom Summerscale was her killer.

'Was Mr Summerscale ever violent towards you?' the prosecutor asked.

'No. Yes. Once,' she responded. 'He hit me once, just once.'

'How did that happen?' the prosecutor asked.

'He believed that he was not the father of our child.'

The silence in the room was absolute. Summerscale looked stunned. His lips trembled for a moment, then sagged on one side as though he had just suffered a stroke. Allaoui muttered something that sounded like a curse in Arabic.

'And was he?'

'He wasn't,' said Natalia.

'Who was?' insisted the prosecutor.

'That is not relevant,' interrupted the judge, who looked as smitten by her as I ever was.

The longer I knew her, the less I understood her power to bewitch men, although – it seemed – only the man who married her somehow managed to escape her spell. For Summerscale, she was not the great prize that Roman Gorsky dreamed her to be. She was not even enough.

'So, if he hit you, how could you say that he is not violent?' the prosecutor ploughed on.

'Because he isn't a violent man,' she repeated. 'I tested him beyond endurance. I deserved to be hit.'

Thus the scales tipped against Summerscale. Gery's

testimony did not help either, although she balanced the evidence by describing him as a gregarious character, a life-enhancing man. Her insights helped corroborate the claim that Summerscale was a cocaine addict – a detail that Natalia seemed to have had no idea about – and it was she who knew for certain something that I had for a long time only suspected: that Allaoui provided the drugs. She also knew that Summerscale punched Natalia that day when we all gathered at their pool, and not just punched, but shoved and kicked her while she was on the floor. She carried a bruise on her lower back for several weeks. Gery had massaged her back to health.

'Do you know why he punched her?' asked the prosecutor.

'I do,' she said. 'He was jealous of Gorsky. He believed that Roman Gorsky was Daisy's father.'

Although it had no apparent link with Janice Allaoui's death, the public revelation of the connection between Roman Gorsky and Natalia Summerscale overshadowed everything else: Tom Summerscale's complex love life, his violence, his cocaine habit, even the jury's eventual decision that he was guilty. When she heard the verdict, Natalia looked like an exhumed corpse. Allaoui, though clearly triumphant at being exonerated, declined an opportunity to give a press statement. Tom Summerscale screamed; a strange, strangled, low-pitched scream, which sounded as though he was gurgling his own blood.

I was hit by a wave of unexpected grief, the like of which I had felt neither when my parents died nor when I lost my country.

10

While Gorsky's body rested in the freezer in the hospital on Fulham Road, the Barracks descended into chaos. The rumours about the estate started circulating immediately. Some papers wrote that he had billions, some that he had no money at all. The cable news channel owned by a rival oligarch claimed that he was worth only twenty thousand pounds on the day he died, and that he had bequeathed the sum to an Israeli charity. If that was true, I thought, the great Gorsky was almost poorer than me.

I had never witnessed him in action in any kind of business, unless one counted the library commission, but I now saw – from the immensity of the vacuum that he left in his wake – just how powerful he must have been. Victor spoke of dozens of *condottieri* around the world – powerful men appointed by Gorsky, CEOs, fund and asset managers, who individually possessed as much money as many British people in the Top One Hundred list. Perhaps because a murder was involved, not one of them dared step in to take immediate charge. He seemed to employ more housekeeping staff in an array of different houses than a major hotel chain. There were hundreds of unpaid contractors, including the famous Xiulan Xi. There were thousands of employees in his businesses all over the planet facing an uncertain future.

The police issued appeals to anyone who might recognise the murderer on the basis of his distinctive gait and not so distinctive white trainers. There were trails, but they ran cold, one after another. Whoever the man was, it was assumed he must be hundreds of miles away. The web became drunk on conspiracy theories about the reasons for Gorsky's death.

Meanwhile The Laurels remained shuttered and apparently empty. Natalia had supposedly left the country the day after her husband was convicted, but I had no idea where she was. The windows of Gery's council flat stayed as resolutely dark as those of The Laurels. Summerscale was in Brixton prison, trying, with the help of his first father-in-law – if the newspapers were to be believed – to find the God he'd last heard about in his school chapel.

Then I received an unexpected e-mail from Gery. I had often seen her texting busily, and laughing over pictures she received on her crystal-encrusted mobile telephone, but we had never communicated in this way before. Her message contained only the simplest of greetings, and an attachment with a photograph: Natalia, Daisy and she, in a cemetery near Montreux, visiting Vladimir Nabokov's grave. It was an outing organised by Natalia, Gery said. One would have expected her to explain what they were doing in Switzerland, but instead she explained Nabokov. He was a famous Russian writer, she said. It looked like a photo of someone's funeral. I responded by asking a volley of questions. I received an automated reply that left me none the wiser, then, some hours later, a simple message in Bulgarian, without a sign-off.

'*Still crying*', it read. There was a single, forlorn, frustrating x for a kiss.

The night Summerscale was convicted, Gery came over to my cottage. I was surprised to see her at my door. It was, and I can't quite explain why, the first time she had called like that. We made love at her place, or we went out. I never invited her over and she never showed any desire to see how I lived. Now she walked in and almost immediately set about tidying up, arranging my books into neat piles, picking up bits of paper, removing and then washing used coffee and tea cups which dotted the place.

I did not try to stop her. I realised that her need to create order in my living space came from some deeper derangement, some less controllable sense of chaos. She was dressed in a pair of old black trousers and a grey cardigan. There was, unusually, not a trace of make-up on her face. Her black hair was plaited, and the plait swung heavily from one side of her back to the other as she worked, like a thick silk cord. She had left her shoes by the door as she came in, and she now shuffled around in a pair of tiny black socks. She saw me looking at her feet and she said, as if to forestall a reaction to some imperfection I had not even noticed: 'Too many hard landings, my love.'

I was surprised to hear myself addressed like that. Perhaps the words meant less in Bulgarian.

Finally, and with everything tidied away, she sat next to me and we looked out towards the unlit windows of the Barracks as the night thickened around us. Natalia did not know what to do with herself, Gery told me. It seemed impossible to leave Tom, and impossible to divorce him now that he was in prison; the reason to abandon him had vanished as well. It seemed impossible to stay in London a day longer, but everywhere else seemed just as bad, or worse. And she couldn't even talk about Gorsky. If you so much as mentioned him, she screamed. The only thing she wanted, Gery said, was to die. But she couldn't do that either. Not with Daisy.

'Poor girl,' Gery shivered. 'And now all this money. How could she be happy?'

I wasn't sure whether she was speaking about Daisy or Natalia. I struggled to understand. She had been speaking to me in Bulgarian all evening, and that was different too, for she had always addressed me in English.

I had never seen her cry before. Now she did. At first her face contorted with the effort, as though she was trying to squeeze the tears out and did not know how. I wrapped my arms around her. Another shiver ran through her like electric current. She took my arm off her shoulder.

'Dear little Nikolai,' she said. 'You don't want to know how good you are. It won't help either of us.'

I was accustomed to having my decisions made for me in this way. I was used to strong women. The Bulgarian was perhaps the strongest of them all.

Fynch, who had by a stroke of luck cashed the last of Gorsky's cheques only a couple of days before the murder, declared that we would use the money to organise Gorsky's funeral as soon as the body was released. Since there seemed to be no next of kin able to fulfil the duty, it was, he said, the decent thing to do in return for all the money he had spent on, and in, the shop. Victor joined in, wanting to do 'the decent thing'. He had organised every conceivable aspect of Russian life in London but he hadn't organised a death, he said.

Had it been possible, we would have followed the Jewish custom and buried him the following day. Instead it was going to be a cremation, followed by a memorial service. We arranged the latter in a synagogue off Edgware Road, one of several he had endowed. It was a liberal, accommodating sort of place, and Victor knew someone who knew the rabbi well. We had no idea how many people would turn up for the service, or for the reception that was supposed to follow it, so we catered generously for three hundred, as many as the synagogue would hold.

Far too generously, in the event. We feared the prurient, and we expected at least some of those hundreds who had availed themselves of Gorsky's hospitality, yet something must have held people back. Now there was nothing for anyone to gain any more to offset a fear of publicity and its negative associations, or fear full stop, for who knew what an oligarch's obsequies could bring. Fynch, Victor and I were the only mourners and none of us was Jewish.

When it became clear that no one else was going to show up, the rabbi, whose open-mindedness about the rite might have been stretched to its limit by a congregation consisting of two Anglicans and a Serbian Orthodox Christian, dispatched the woman cantor to summon a small group of elderly men and women away from some business that they had been pursuing in the bowels of the building. The group stuck together and kept a polite distance, seemingly as bewildered as we were in the echoing emptiness of the temple. At least they knew the form. Fynch, Victor and I waited for the instructions, shuffled the service booklets, holding them back to front, then upside down. We read the words of the Kaddish and lit the candles for Gorsky's soul.

It was difficult to think of a more impersonal service. No one knew enough about the man to make it less so. Fynch read a speech about the Russian love of books. Victor recited a poem by Pushkin in a soft, lilting Cambridge Russian. That sound moved me more than anything else. It echoed with unexpected losses, a sadness well beyond the life we were mourning. I imagined Victor as an undergraduate struggling with Russian declensions inside some medieval quad and I remembered myself poring over *Paradise Lost* at the other end of the continent, trying desperately to make sense of both the English language and the verse, and then I saw Gorsky as a young academic – much further north – explaining a long algorithm while his students whispered the news of 'glasnost' and 'perestroika'. I beheld the promise of a shiny new world which had been contained in those two clunky words.

The rabbi, a solemn man whose Polish father had arrived in Britain on the *Kindertransport*, spoke of the pogroms, of Russian Jews escaping to Britain and America, then of the kindness of Britain towards its Jews, which had evolved with fewer recent blemishes than elsewhere in Europe, although even here, as one went backwards, the story darkened. He had seen Gorsky in the temple only once or twice, but Gorsky had invested a substantial sum in the *bimah* that he stood on as he read. This generous man, who was most likely not a believer, the rabbi said, was perhaps a tormented soul. It was a pity he did not allow anyone near him.

A lanky dark-haired woman, looking like a young Joan Baez, appeared and sang mournfully, *a cappella*, a Yiddish song which spoke of calves being led to slaughter. It made as much or as little sense as the rest of the ceremony. I stared at the empty seats. The dark neo-Byzantine space around us was architecturally close enough to the nave of an Orthodox church to make me feel at home and at ease, yet the absence of familiar images of saints and angels was somehow in keeping with the loneliness of the man whose life we were trying to celebrate.

Afterwards, we all stood for a while in a small circle around a mountain of smoked salmon, not knowing what to say to each other. Fynch and I took a couple of unopened bottles of champagne away – leaving dozens to the rabbi and the men and women of Gorsky's forlorn rent-a-minyan – and emerged, blinking, into the late afternoon on Edgware Road. The owner of the Syrian shop next door stepped out and held up a tray of plump, glistening dates.

'*Orqod fi salaam,*' he said, bowing slightly. 'May his soul rest in peace.'

He knew where we had just been and why. Further down the street, men sat in sheesha cafes in animated groups while women covered in black from head to toe shopped for sweetmeats and syrups in grocery stores that spilled onto the pavements in shiny waves of oranges, pomegranates and watermelons. The sounds and smells of the Middle East closed around us like the sea, as though the man who grew up on the snowy banks of the Neva, the man whose death we had just lamented, had never existed at all.

I was the one who, seven days later, disposed of his ashes. I upturned a Siberian malachite urn above the Thames on the spot where he died. I was not alone. Not long after the memorial service, a tiny woman, looking like a baby crow under a wide-brimmed black hat, had arrived at the Barracks with one of Gorsky's bodyguards. It was practically my last day in the gatekeeper's lodge. I watched her slow progress as she paused every now and then to wipe her eyes or blow her nose. Half an hour later, the same man who had accompanied her knocked on my door to say that Roman Gorsky's mother, Elizaveta Alexandrovna Stern, who had just arrived in London, wondered if I would mind joining her for tea.

Her frail body was as lost in an ornate antique armchair as she was lost in her son's vast palace and in this strange town which he had, for reasons she still failed to grasp, chosen as his home among all the cities in the world.

'Fate,' she kept repeating in a slow, deliberate Russian, translating her own sentences into a heavily accented and equally deliberate but faultless French. 'He said he was following his fate. Paris, I would understand. Rome too. Or Berlin and Vienna. Even Zurich or Helsinki . . . but London . . . I am not sure I do. He spoke French and German. His English was very poor.'

I assured her that wasn't the case. I spoke in an imperfect mix of the two languages she was using, for, although I understood them reasonably well, I was very far from conversant in either. I peppered my speech with words from my mother tongue, which was similar enough to Russian to help her grasp my meaning. She reminded me of my own mother. Her hands, speckled with the liver spots of old age, kept clasping and reclasping each other. They were just as bird-like as the rest of her. It took some effort to believe that she could have given birth to someone like Roman Gorsky. She was dark and her small eyes were inky and shiny, like currants. And she did not look wealthy. She wore a plain black dress decorated with a simple amber brooch the like of which you could get for a few roubles in any Russian market. On her feet, which barely skimmed the floor as she sat, she wore a pair of small-girl's polished boots, totally unsuited to the summer weather.

It was heartbreaking that she did not make it for the funeral service, she said, but it was already becoming obvious to me that she had indirectly allowed it to happen. She did not want to mourn him with his so-called friends, or be photographed for the world to see. She could not understand so many things about the way her son had chosen to lead his life. When the news of his death reached her, she did not even possess a passport. She had never needed it, she said. Tragic, but also better perhaps: she did not believe in all that synagogue business. She was a Communist. That is why, although she loved Roman and although he was a loving son, she steadfastly refused his money. Her ageing comrades now went hungry and cold on their miserable pensions. How could she face them in some luxuriously equipped apartment? She urged Roman to give his wealth away to the needy. The only God she believed in, she explained, was the common good of the human race.

'Roman too,' she added. 'He was a good, hard-working boy, a Communist himself. He lived modestly. And he did not believe in any of that religious stuff. Sorry if you are a believer, if what I say offends you. I know that there are few of us left and that many think faith is important if we are not to disappear completely, but it is not so.'

She clearly thought I was Jewish.

'And Roman agreed with me. He was proud of being Russian. And I was proud of him. I was honoured to be his mother.

'I was honoured to be his mother,' she repeated

when we stood by the Thames, just the two of us on the spot where his life came to its abrupt end, watched over at a distance by one of Roman's bodyguards, and the enormous golden Buddha from the Battersea side. I opened the urn and upended it above the water. A plume of pale powder rose into the air and slowly descended into the murky water, pooling briefly then disappearing under the surface. The guard crossed himself with a quick hand movement. A horn sounded from a barge somewhere to the east. Elizaveta Stern stood next to me, now nursing the empty malachite jar with its golden Romanov eagles like the swaddled body of a baby. I did not dare ask whether she knew she had a granddaughter. I had to leave the revelation – if such it was – to Natalia and her conscience. Elizaveta's husband was long dead and she had lost her only child. She sighed, deeply, but did not cry.

When the final strange twist to this story happened ten months later, at first it seemed like another case of random street violence. There was a robbery in Elgin Crescent in Notting Hill. A woman was forced to surrender an expensive watch at knifepoint, and a passer-by, an off-duty soldier, tackled the robber. The criminal, a Tunisian, was a small-time drug dealer who turned to mugging to support his own drug habit after his employer and supplier was jailed for drug-related offences. The man's distinctive gait and an unusual card case in which he had stashed a few wraps of heroin provided incriminating evidence which helped solve an earlier, much more serious crime. He thought the case a worthless trinket – the pawnbroker had refused him a loan for thirty pounds against it. It was a Fabergé.

When he was challenged about the way it came to be in his possession, his confession was as quick as it was baffling. He had taken it from the pocket of Janice Allaoui's English lover. He had killed them both, he claimed. Mahmoud Allaoui, his boss, had ordered her murder, but he did not have to order anything. He killed Mrs Allaoui because he had wanted to kill her anyway. Mrs Allaoui – Janice – had been his mistress. He loved Janice and Janice loved him. She was the love of his life. Life without her was torture. They planned an escape to the sun, a hotel on the Tunisian coast which they would run together one day. She kept promising to leave Mahmoud, but she kept lying. Then Mahmoud, suspecting nothing, revealed in his anger that Janice had another lover, an Englishman. The Tunisian confronted her. He threatened to kill her if she did not supply her lover's address: he was going to lie in wait and beat up the bastard. She obeyed, and she promised to leave Allaoui for him yet again, but he killed the whore anyway. If she could not be his alone, she was not going to be anyone's. She did not deserve to live. Of course she let him into the flat; they had been meeting there regularly. She said that she was the cleaner but to him she was a paid whore.

Having killed Janice, he stalked The Laurels over several days. His rage and his fear about being found out only grew. He saw the Englishman with his wife several times. Late one night, he saw him kissing her on the doorstep, he followed him and he killed him. They have everything they want, those men, and then they want other people's wives too, he said, as though he was the wronged party. No, he did not know anything about anyone called Roman Gorsky. He saw his victim's face clearly. It was the same man whom he had watched going in and out of that house and whom he had seen that very evening on the doorstep, kissing his wife. He killed an Englishman, he was absolutely certain, not a Russian, and certainly not a Jew. No, definitely not a Jew.

On the day I finally moved out of the gatekeeper's cottage, Summerscale was exonerated and the Barracks went up for sale for several hundred million pounds, an insignificant slice, it transpired, of the fortune Gorsky had left to Daisy Summerscale. There was a fortune after all.

It was also the day I met Natalia for the last time.

I had taken a short let in Mile End, a flat-share with an MA student at the LSE. The fact that I could barely afford to share an apartment with a Greek boy in his early twenties spoke volumes about my position. I had spent more than a decade in Britain living like mistletoe, attaching myself to the branches of powerful oaks. That decade was over and I had nothing to my name.

I hired a small van with a merry Romanian driver who

came all the way from Edmonton to Chelsea and was ready to drive east. He parked off-street, by the ornate gate. He now leaned against his battered vehicle and whistled through a gap left behind one of his lower incisors, while studying the astonishing edifice through the ornate railings. I carried my boxes into the van. He wasn't planning to do any heavy lifting for the pittance I was paying. When I mentioned that the palace was Russian-owned he nodded, as though he had suspected as much. That was the way the world had been ordered for his entire life.

He halted – mid tune – when Natalia emerged from her own massive gateway across the road, parting the traffic on her way over. She was carrying a small hamper. To make sure that I would have something for dinner wherever I was going, she said. She clearly knew more about my movements than I did about hers, for I had not realised she was back in London until that moment. I invited her upstairs, into the now empty room from which, over the past months, I had watched Gorsky's palace being dismantled and rebuilt again just for her. We stood facing each other uncertainly, like two actors rehearsing the final act of a Chekhov play, when everything that was supposed to happen had already happened and the characters were departing one by one.

She looked as though she hadn't slept in months. It occurred to me that we had never had what one could describe as a proper conversation. I fetched a book from one of my boxes, a cheap paperback. It was a Soviet art history book which used to belong to Gorsky long before I started compiling his library. I stole it from his shelves the day after his murder.

I already knew I needed no mementos. There was no way to forget him.

An ex libris bookplate inside the front cover had the initials RBG pencilled in, and, in the corner, an old-style Leningrad telephone number. A few of the inside pages still carried his scribbled annotations: asterisked names of artists with 'Natasha mentioned,' or 'as explained by Tasha' or 'liked by Talya'. He had many pet names for her, as Russians do, but I don't remember him ever addressing her by any of them.

There was something poignant about the earnestness

with which he had clearly studied the book. I imagined, from the year of its publication, that she must have told him stories of her art degree in their early encounters, and that he had followed the references up. His entire life seemed guided by the desire to capture and harness everything she was fond of, to recreate the world in the image of her dreams so that she would desire no one but him.

She briefly pored over the book, touching the yellowing oblong of the ex libris bookplate, then leafed through pages of black-and-white photographs, some of them of artists in rooms very much like those she must have grown up in, in the city that was once called Stalingrad. She was as beautiful as ever, but she was no longer an alien princess. In fact, she reminded me of several of the girls I had known at school in Belgrade. It seemed strange that I hadn't noticed the likeness before.

'These pictures take me back,' she said, as if she had guessed my thoughts. 'There were months when we existed on potato soup alone. Not just my family, the whole town. The entire country. But I wasn't unhappy there, just thirsty to see the world and sometimes frustrated by general poverty. I understood very early on how important it was to have plenty of money, because money made things possible and shielded you from so much. I am sure you understand that.'

I did not understand. I had never thought money shielded you from anything.

'When Roman arrived in Volgograd for my father's funeral,' Natalia said just before I proffered that parting gift, 'he refused even to acknowledge my presence, let alone speak to me. I had just arrived from London on a long connecting flight. There was a sudden snowstorm, then four hours' delay in Moscow while they cleared the runway and de-iced the plane. I felt shell-shocked and disoriented. I had been married to Tom for a while at that stage. I was always fond of Tom and I was not unhappy with him, but I had wanted to escape Russia so much and for such a long time that I did not know what to do with myself in London when homesickness struck. I had no friends in England then, not even someone like Gery to keep me company. The English just watched me, like a giraffe in a zoo. When Tom was away, as he was a lot at that stage, I paced up and down the Mayfair apartment we were living in and I cried all the time. Then my father died and I was convinced that I had killed him, that my marriage was the cause of his heart attack. He hated Tom. He hated Britain. He had other ideas for me.

'There were all these old men at his funeral, old Communists in bad suits, with gold teeth under their moustaches and endless rows of medals, frail and doddery, but glad to be among old comrades and still with the self-confidence born of having exercised power in the prime of their lives. They were burying Dad but they might as well have been burying an entire era, everything they had ever stood for, everything their reputations depended on. They looked at me as though I was the enemy.

'No-one spoke to me, not even my mother. I understood Roman: we had parted in very unhappy circumstances. I couldn't understand the others. I kept sending money to them all. I wondered if I should have stayed away.

'Then a comrade of my father's who had been Brezhnev's secretary delivered the funeral oration. He spoke at length about my father's life and achievements. All I could think of, all I could see, from the moment he opened his mouth, was the coffin which ferried the body of Sergey, my eldest brother, from Afghanistan. It is one of my earliest memories; the touch of zinc still seemed cold from its journey in the underbelly of a plane, under the red flag. I was too young to mourn my brother, too young even to remember him properly. They called them *black tulips*, those planes. When I was a child, I did not know this. I looked at the atlas to see where Seryozha had fought. I thought his soul had floated on black petals, across the Caspian Sea, across the Urals, all the way back to us. A heavily framed photograph, showing his young face gazing out forever above the striped paratroopers' *telnyashka* he was so proud to wear, became for us an atheist icon. In my school, which had been his school too, there was another picture, of my father receiving a medal on his son's behalf from this same man. Now my father was dead too, yet here he was, this comrade, this friend of his, ancient and stooped but still brimming with the will to live.

'Comrade Volkov was one of those men who made the

Soviet Union great, he said. The workers of the world had never been as oppressed as they are now, at the beginning of this new millennium, and imperialists think that they have triumphed. But, don't deceive yourselves, he said, and looked at me: the ideal of Communism is not dead. The oppressed proletariat will rise again and the new revolution will be even more glorious than the last one. Then there will be no rich and poor, for there will be no property and no money anywhere on this planet. Its riches will belong to everyone equally. From everyone according to their abilities, to everyone according to their needs, Comrade Marx wrote. That is how Comrade Volkov lived, a Marxist-Leninist in thought and deed to the end of his days. His abilities were immeasurable, his needs were modest to the very end, he said. He finished his speech and stood to attention before the coffin. There was a large wreath of white winter roses on it, with a five-pointed star, in red carnations, in its centre.

'Then they played an army march Dad loved, "The Farewell of Slavianka", and I could no longer fight back tears. My heart was overflowing with pity for them and for their world, yet they looked at me as though they had somehow defeated me. Then Roman suddenly came over to me and put his arm around my shoulder.

'"*Nu, nu*, Natasha," he whispered, "*Nu, nu*, my little one. You must never cry, my love. When you cry, the world stops making sense."'

She fell silent for a while in the empty room. I had no heart to ask about her plans for the future; she seemed too bewildered to have any. I was trying to make sense of her confession. The telling details and her tone took me aback more than the revelations it contained. I could hear the Romanian outside, turning the van for its journey east, then honking once or twice. There was a little stub of a pencil on the floor and Natalia bent down to pick it up. She rolled it on her palm for a while, examining it, then put it in her pocket. She added one final, by now unsurprising, sentence to her story:

'The following day I flew back to Moscow and then on to London to my husband, but it was on that evening that my daughter was conceived.'

11

I bought back my parents' apartment in Belgrade for a sum much lower than I had sold it for fifteen years earlier, smaller in numerical as well as real terms. The property market has been dead here for years. You can buy an entire town for less than the price of Gorsky's palace. No-one buys. No one sells. No one has any money.

I run an English language school for children whose parents dream of Natalia Summerscale's lifestyle for their progeny, who dream of money and escape. I have a girlfriend, a local girl and an English teacher, fifteen years younger than me. We have been living together for over two years. She visited London once. She tells me that she walked from her hotel in Bloomsbury all the way down to Piccadilly and on into Mayfair. When she came to the edges of Hyde Park, she assumed that there was nothing worth seeing beyond it and turned back.

She doesn't want to revisit England, which is fine by me. She is tired of Europe, she says. She talks of India, Nepal and Bhutan, and she quotes nuggets of New Age wisdom about the purpose of life and the secret of happiness. She does not envy anyone, because envy is toxic, she says. It eats the vessel it is stored in. She cycles, and she does yoga, and she aligns her chakras. She breathes in deeply, she holds her breath, and she exhales.

In the mornings, I run by the Danube to keep fit. In the evenings, I sit by it with a glass of local wine in one of the many cafes that line its banks, watching its waters flow endlessly towards the Black Sea.

I read a bit, after work, though nowhere near as much as I used to. I am about to finish Macaulay's *History of England*. Before that I read a book about big game hunting which took several weeks. I can't remember its author. I gave the volume away. We have no library because we de-clutter religiously. My girlfriend has pinned a card above my desk which reads: *Do not be afraid to let go*. She is still a child. How can she know that I had, for a long time, found it impossible to hold onto things?

When I think of London now, I think of Gorsky. London was once an imperial city, then it was, for a while, just another European capital with good museums and bad hotels, inhabited by a nation that was once capable of great things. Finally the city unmoored itself from its nation and became a home to arrivals from all over the world, best suited to those who had millions and those who had nothing. People like Gorsky made it temporarily a great Russian city, the second St Petersburg, the new Moscow. Their children, now being educated in expensive British boarding schools, will never know the same thirst. In time, they too will become like the English. The new conquerors will come from India and China, to spend and to buy as the Russians did. The city will be their lover for a moment, then give herself to the next wave.

Strange to say, but I am at peace. My girlfriend talks about the power of now, about the importance of keeping your thoughts anchored in the present. Neither the past nor the future exists. To please her, I sit next to her on her yoga mat and, far from the sea, we meditate together to the pre-recorded sound of the waves. I follow her prompts. I inhale as deeply as I can, I hold my breath, I let go. I close my eyes and I see a plume of white powder floating over the Thames. The world stands still.

A NOTE ABOUT THE NOVEL

No reader can have got this far without realising the debt I owe to F. Scott Fitzgerald's *Great Gatsby*, but I still wish to record my gratitude. Readers familiar with Russian literature will have noticed references to a list of writers and poets too long to repeat. Their works have been a home from home all my life. Natalia Summerscale picks up the stub of a pencil in the empty room at the end of *Gorsky* because that room is filled to the brim with the spirit of Anton Chekhov and I feel for her.

Although Gorsky is a Russian name with variants in many Slavonic languages, my inspiration came from my mother tongue. Very early on, while I was searching for the requisite echo of Gatsby, I remembered the title of the great nineteenth-century epic, *Gorski Vijenac* ('*The Mountain Wreath*') by the Montenegrin Prince-Bishop Petar Petrović-Njegoš. The association seemed fortuitous. Njegoš was ordained bishop in St Petersburg in 1833. In 1837 he prayed on Pushkin's grave at Sviatogorsky Monastery in southern Russia, and he dedicated a collection of his verse to Pushkin. No one can overstate the depth of Montenegrin and Serbian feeling for Russian culture.

As a one-time Serbian medievalist, I was also influenced by the rather appropriate name of the great Belgrade-based Byzantinist, George Ostrogorsky (with its suggestion of eastern-Gorsky), who was himself from St Petersburg.

There is another Gorsky in the making. A doctoral student of mine, Nebojša Radić, is writing a novel which couldn't be more different from this. It does, however, have a character called Alex Gorsky. We discussed the coincidence when he sent me his first chapters. I did not want Alex to change his name. It is perhaps proof of our shared Serbian origins and interest in Russia, linked by some Jungian correspondence of thought.

It could be argued that my main character is not Roman Gorsky but London. It is the city in which I have lived, and which I have loved, for almost thirty years. The London of *Gorsky*, however, is a place of imagined details. The Laurels and the Barracks do not exist, and neither does Fynch's bookshop (although I very much wish it did). Many other places and all of the main characters are similarly fictional: this is, after all, a novel.

I am fortunate to count both native Russians and Russian scholars and experts among my friends, but I have not consulted them, and they are not to blame for anything that may be wrong with this book's portrayal of Russia and its people, any more than my London friends are for my take on our city. For what is right with it, I am grateful to my editor Clara Farmer, my agent Faith Evans, and my first reader, as always, Simon Goldsworthy.